SIXTH-GRADE HIGH

Other Apple paperbacks you will enjoy:

Millicent the Magnificent
by Candice F. Ransom

There's One in Every Family
by Candice F. Ransom

Amanda the Cut-up
by Vivian Schurfranz

A Cry in the Night
by Carol Ellis

Living with Dad
by Lynn Z. Helm

SIXTH-GRADE HIGH

Candice F. Ransom

AN
APPLE
PAPERBACK

SCHOLASTIC INC.
New York Toronto London Auckland Sydney

ISBN 0-590-43891-3

12 11 10 9 8 7 6 5 4   3 4 5 6/9

Printed in the U.S.A.   40

First Scholastic printing, August 1991

SIXTH-GRADE HIGH

1

"Expect the worst, especially when you have a weird family."
— *Maxie Granville's Theory of Life*, Vol. II

Our annual backyard Labor Day picnic was winding down. To celebrate the last day of summer vacation we had a no-holds-barred cookout. Mom made baked beans and potato salad and deviled eggs. "Forget cholesterol, forget diets. Forget lettuce!" she declared. Dad grilled hot dogs and hamburgers. We ate until we were stuffed, then everybody sat around in the backyard.

To look at us, you'd think we'd stepped out of a Norman Rockwell painting — "Typical American Family Celebrates Labor Day." Actually only *one* of us was what you'd call normal. The others — my parents and my brother, Todd — *appeared* normal, but they really weren't. Or else they'd be as worried as I was about the first day of school.

Mom and Dad talked about Mom's new book-store. Mom stripped thorns from roses and idly tucked the flowers behind her ear. Dad nibbled on leftover potato salad, even though he was trying to lose a few pounds. Todd lazed in a lounge chair, quiet for once, and read the latest issue of *Surfer* magazine.

I sat in the other lounge chair at the far end of the patio with my *Theory of Life* notebook opened in my lap. I wasn't writing, though. I was trying to figure out how I was going to survive sixth grade at Centreville High School.

It didn't seem possible that summer was over. Technically it was still summer by the calendar, but it was over for me. The first day of school was the first day of fall, by *my* calendar.

I couldn't believe that Dilys and I wouldn't be biking to the pool tomorrow, or over to the mall for a frozen yogurt. Instead we'll be trotting off to *high school*, which was the most impossible thought of all.

Nobody else seemed the least bit bothered by the fact that I, Maxie Granville, age eleven, was going to *high school* the very next day. They chatted about the store and the sunset as if the world wasn't going to stop in less than twenty-four hours. Todd asked Dad if he could have a body board. Dad asked Todd why he wanted to strap his perfectly good body to a board. Todd gave up temporarily.

Finally Mom and Dad started cleaning up the picnic mess. Mom gathered cups and plates while Dad rinsed the barbecue grill.

"School tomorrow," Mom said mildly, like she'd only just remembered. Dilys told me yesterday that *her* mother had been counting the hours since June.

Suddenly the hose shut off. "Picture time!" Dad exclaimed. "Todd, Maxie. Over here on the bench."

I groaned. "Oh, Dad. Do we have to?"

He raced around, getting the camera into position. "Yes, Maxie, we have to. For posterity we must have a record of this fabulous picnic, our way of honoring America's work force, to whom this day is dedicated. A day in which the working class can rest from its labors — "

"Except the one who did most of the cooking," Mom put in wryly.

"Great job, Mom," Todd said, ambling over to the bench. "C'mon, Moondoggie. Get over here."

He meant me. My brother was obsessed with surfing. When he was not welded to his skateboard, Todd could be found at the Wavedancer shop at the mall. Why he yearned to ride the wild surf was beyond me. We lived in the suburbs of

3

northern Virginia, about as far from the California surfing scene as you can get. We've never even been to California. Todd would shove off for Malibu in a heartbeat, except he's only fourteen. Some days, like now, I wished he *would* go.

As I sat down on the bench, he sang, "Moondoggie, Moondoggie. Get along, little Moondoggie."

"Don't call me that," I said, swatting him. "You know I hate it." "Moondoggie" was the name of some character on the old *Gidget* movies Todd rented from the video store.

"Moondoggie, Moondoggie — "

"Mo-om! Make him stop!"

"Don't tease your sister," Mom said, adjusting the roses in her hair.

"Are we ready?" Dad asked. He set the timer, then rushed back to sit with us.

Before Dad got a camera with a tripod, we'd pile on the sofa while Dad held the camera out at arm's length and snapped the shutter with his thumb. In those photographs, we looked like we'd had our heads knocked together, and our noses were always a mile too big because of the way Dad had to hold the camera. Then Mom bought him a better camera with a tripod. But instead of the pictures getting better, they got worse.

"Can we look like regular people this time?" I said.

4

"Oh, Maxie," Dad said indulgently. "We're not posing for an executive portrait. It's okay for families to be silly. Here goes! Everybody say 'Englebert Humperdinck!' "

I looked over at my father. He still had on his barbecue apron that said, "I'll Do Anything for Chocolate." Mom crossed her legs like an old-time movie star. The roses drooped in her hair. And Todd — well . . . over red-and-green surfer's jams he had on a Hawaiian shirt printed with parrots and palm trees. He lifted one foot so his acid-green unlaced high-tops would get into the picture, and he grinned like a catfish.

The camera buzzed. The ordeal was over. I hopped up immediately. "That's it, right?" I said hopefully. Dilys was supposed to come over for dessert. I didn't want her to see my family goofing around.

Too late. Dilys Freeman walked into our yard as my parents mugged for a second shot. She stared at them. "Boy, I thought *my* family was weird, but yours really goes over the top."

When Dilys' parents got divorced last year, they divided everything equally, including the children. Dilys lived with her mother two houses from my house, while her older brother lived with their father in an apartment. They even split the pets — Mrs. Freeman got custody of the dog; Mr. Freeman took the cat.

"Speaking of weirdos," Todd said sarcastically. Dilys stuck out her tongue at him, though she should have been used to people making cracks about her outfits by now.

Today she had on black bicycle shorts, an oversized Banana Republic T-shirt, low black boots, and a wristful of neon rubber bracelets.

Dilys and I shared the chaise lounge. My mother brought dessert over to us.

"Is your mom dropping by?" my mother asked Dilys, handing her a piece of blueberry pie topped with vanilla ice cream.

"Thanks," Dilys said, taking the plate. "Mom said to tell you she's sorry but she can't make it. She's got a lot to do." To me, she added, "She's probably laying her clothes out for work tomorrow."

Dilys thought it was terrible that her mother set her clothes out for the next day. "She plans every single instant!" she complained to me more than once. I never admitted that I set *my* clothes out for the next day, too, at least on school nights. I hated rushing around in the morning. But Dilys would never understand. She always looked like she grabbed any old thing and threw it on.

My best friend was a nonconformist. She announced this fact the first time I saw her waiting at the bus stop. We were both second-graders that year. I was already entranced with Dilys' long black hair and gray eyes, so different from my plain brown hair. I thought she was telling me her religion, and at the dinner table that night I asked my father what church nonconformists went to. He laughed so hard he sprayed coffee all over the table, and then told me what the word meant. A nonconformist is somebody who doesn't follow the crowd.

A few days later, I was playing with my Barbie doll at the edge of the woods behind our house. I saw Dilys standing in a patch of weeds nearby, a towel pinned around her shoulders like a cape. With a set of watercolor paints, she seemed to be painting the scarlet leaves of a dogwood tree.

"What are you doing?" I asked, curious.

"I'm the Fall Fairy," she said, completely serious. "I paint the leaves yellow and red and gold."

I noticed her brush wasn't even wet. She sort of wiped it dryly over a leaf. But I was fascinated all the same.

"Can I help?" I begged. "Please? I have an old set of paints."

She regarded me with cool gray eyes. "Okay. You can be my assistant. Paint those leaves yellow."

With a "brush" of twigs and my dried-up watercolors, I eagerly set to work. It never occurred me that I was only the Fall Fairy's *assistant*. I was happy to have a new friend. We had just

7

moved to Virginia from Wisconsin. Todd, who was ten at the time, had made friends right away with some boys down the street. But I rode my bike and explored in the vacant lot behind our house, wishing for somebody to play with.

Dilys Freeman became my best friend. She was definitely the leader. I didn't mind being the follower because her ideas were always better than mine.

If Dilys was a nonconformist, I was a realist. I faced facts and did all the worrying nobody else in my family ever bothered to do. Right now, though, I was really worried about school the next day.

The Letter came last Monday. I happened to bring in the mail that day. When I saw the envelope marked Willow Springs Elementary in the upper left-hand corner, I thought it was my room assignment. I took the mail to my mother, who was in the kitchen going over an inventory list for the bookstore she and her friend Lola had recently opened. She slit the envelope and read the letter.

"Well," she said, with raised eyebrows. "This is a surprise."

"What?" Maybe my fifth-grade teacher made a mistake and I had not been passed to sixth grade after all.

"Maxie, you'll be going to Centreville High this year."

8

"Oh, Mom." Sometimes my parents made awful jokes. Everybody but me has a strange sense of humor in my family.

"I'm not kidding," she insisted. "It seems the new addition to Willow Springs Elementary isn't going to be finished in time. Your school is over-crowded with all the new people moving into the area, so they are sending the sixth-graders to the high school this year."

The woods behind our house are gone now. Developers had bulldozed the trees and built big new houses. Families moved in every day, it seemed. That was why Dilys and I and all the other kids in our class were being sent to high school.

Mom read me the incredible details. The sixth-graders would be bused to Centreville High, which was one block over from Willow Springs Elementary. The high school was only a year old, and not up to "full capacity yet," whatever that meant. So instead of installing the sixth grade in drafty trailers behind the elementary school, they decided to ship us to the high school. We'd still be part of Willow Springs Elementary. We would go back to Willow Springs for assemblies and special programs. But we would spent our days at Centreville High, sharing lockers, the gym, and the cafeteria with the big kids.

"Won't that be exciting?" Mom concluded.

It was not exciting. Not to me, anyway. I wasn't

9

ready to go to high school, even as a sixth-grader. I hadn't had any practice at high school! I hadn't even been to *junior* high.

"It's not fair," I said to Dilys now, smearing the last bit of blueberry pie around on my plate. "I've looked forward to being a sixth-grader since I was in first grade. The sixth-graders get to do all the neat stuff. It's our reward for slaving five whole years. And look what they've done to us. Kicked us down to the bottom again!"

"True," Dilys agreed. "We'll hardly be number one at Centreville High."

"We won't be *any*thing. It'll be awful, I just know it!"

"My mom is throwing a fit. She doesn't like the idea of her little baby going to sixth grade in a high school," Dilys said disdainfully.

"I don't like it, either," I confessed. "My mom thinks it'll be fun. Why is your mother worried?"

"She's afraid I'll grow up too fast." Dilys made a rude noise. "What did she think the divorce did?"

"My mother thinks it's great because Todd and I will both be in the same school. She says it'll be easier to keep track of us." I drew up my knees, knocking my *Theory of Life* notebook to the ground.

Dilys picked it up. "Are you still working on this?"

I nodded. "I'm on volume two."

The *Theory of Life* book started as a class assignment. Last year in fifth-grade Writing Lab, we wrote books on the school computers. Dilys wrote an autobiography called *My Life, So Far*. Most of the other kids made up stories. I wasn't very creative, so I wrote a collection of things about life that I had observed. I called my book *Maxie Granville's Theory of Life*. Even after the assignment was over, I kept scribbling theories.

"I'm trying to think of a theory about why we're being sent to high school," I said to Dilys.

"There is no theory. They don't have room for us in the old school. Period. Don't worry so much, Maxie. It's just sixth grade in a different building, that's all." She plucked a blade of grass and feathered it with her slim fingers. "You only have to watch out for one thing."

"What?" I said, thinking she was going to tell me the secret to opening lockers.

"Change."

"Change?" I repeated. "What do you mean?"

"Everybody changes in high school. Don't you know anything? My brother changed a lot. I bet that's why my mom is worried about me going."

"What kind of changes?" Suddenly my palms were clammy. I thought I had all my worrying lined up and now Dilys had something new for me to agonize over.

"Well, in Marlowe's case, it was a change for

11

the worse. He became smart-alecky." Dilys shrugged. "I don't know why it happens. It just does. People act differently in high school, for some reason."

I sat up and clutched her arm. "It won't happen to us, will it, Dilys? Let's make a promise to stay exactly the same, okay? I don't want my sixth-grade year ruined any more than it already is."

"Okay," Dilys promised breezily. "We won't change. I don't need to change anyway. I like myself the way I am."

I sat back again, relieved. Sixth grade was going to be traumatic enough without worrying about changing into a new person. Then a thought nagged at one corner of my brain. I remembered the last day of school, when we received end-of-the-year grade cards. Our teacher wrote comments at the bottom of our report cards. *It was a pleasure having Dilys in my class,* the teacher had written on Dilys' card. *She is a bright and creative student, a joy to teach.* On my card, in evident desperation, the teacher put, *Maxie speaks clearly and distinctly. She is neat and clean. I enjoyed having her in my class.*

Dilys scoffed at the comments, but I took them to heart. The nicest thing a teacher could say about me was that I was neat and clean? That I spoke distinctly? I mean, who would want to be remembered for not mumbling?

Dilys liked herself exactly the way she was because she was bright and creative, not a dull stick like me. Maybe, I thought, a *little* change wouldn't hurt. Not too much — I hated radical changes of any kind — but just enough to spice things up.

Dilys stood up and stretched. "I have to go home. Thanks for the pie, Mrs. Granville. It was delish." She clumped across the patio. I didn't know how Dilys could stand wearing boots, as hot as it was. I guess nonconformists don't mind the heat.

"School tomorrow," my mother said again. She sounded happy.

"Smile!" Dad jumped in front of Dilys and snapped her picture. She still had one more member of my family to try to avoid.

Dilys clumped cautiously around Todd. My goofy brother was "walking" his skateboard across the patio, showing off.

"Hey, Dad," he said. "Can I get a body board?"

"What did I answer when you asked me that same question an hour ago?"

"You said no."

"Good memory!" Dad praised. "You should go far. But not on a body board."

"Awwww."

I reached for my notebook to jot down my latest theory of life. My family wasn't the tiniest bit worried about my being sent to high school, and they *should* be. Was it any wonder I was working on my second volume of my *Theory of Life*? I mean, with a family like mine, I certainly couldn't count on *them* to help me figure out life.

I'd have to do it myself.

2

At seven-fifteen the next morning I was on the phone to Dilys.

"I don't know what to wear!" I cried frantically. Neither of the two outfits I had set out the night before seemed right for high school.

"Just wear anything," she said unhelpfully. She sounded scratchy-voiced. I imagined her sitting up in bed, her black hair a tangled mess. I'd been up since six-thirty, pitching stuff out of my closet. Dilys yawned into the receiver, totally unconcerned about our first day at Centreville High.

I should have known better than to ask *her* advice about fashion. Nonconformists don't care about clothes.

I didn't ask my mother's advice, either. She was busy getting Dad off to work. When the weather was nice, he rode his motorbike to the Metro station. He looked so ridiculous, buzzing off to the city in a suit and a red crash helmet. Todd was

15

right behind him. It was his first day at Centreville High, too. He was a freshman at Centreville,
a *legitimate* student, he pointed out, not a *boarder*, like I was. For the occasion, he actually
pressed his grape-patterned jams.

If only the letter of instruction Willow Springs
Elementary sent had had something *useful* in it
besides the name of my teacher and my bus assignments . . . like what to wear and how to fix
my hair!

I wound up putting on one of my two "outfits"
anyway, a short yellow skirt and a yellow-striped
T-shirt. I pulled back one side of my hair and
fastened it with a yellow barrette. Then I burst
into tears.

My mother walked into my room at that unfor-
tunate moment. "Maxie! What's wrong!"

"I look like a banana!"

"No, you don't. You look very nice. Fresh and
cheerful." She smoothed my hair. "Don't fret so
much, dear."

"Wouldn't you worry if you were going to high
school three years early?" It was like one of those
dreams where you're someplace you're not supposed to be, like a grocery store at the bottom of
the ocean. Only this wasn't a dream. It was real.

Mom put her arm around me. "You've been a
bundle of nerves ever since you got the letter." I
was surprised — I didn't think anyone had no-

16

ticed. "Maxie, try to take one day at a time. You'll find life will be easier if you do."

I couldn't even take one minute at a time, I was so keyed up. Barely able to choke down two bites of my breakfast, I raced out to the bus stop. Dilys was already there, indifferently wearing the same clothes she'd had on yesterday.

"Aren't you nervous?" I asked her, wondering if my knapsack was too babyish. Maybe I should have brought Mom's big vinyl tote instead.

"Should I be?" Dilys looked as unmovable as Mount Rushmore. "Maxie, it's only school. You're not interviewing for a job at the Capitol or anything."

When the bus came, we headed straight for the long seat in the back. The bus stopped first at Willow Springs Elementary to let off all the kids except us sixth-graders. We chugged over to our new school on the next block.

My first impression of Centreville High was that it looked a little like a castle and a little like a fortress. It was *huge* — three stories of light-brown square stones. No windows in the front, just a pair of five-sided glass towers that jutted up on either side of the entrance.

"We need a guide!" I exclaimed as we got off the bus.

A group of teachers from Willow Springs Elementary waited by the flagpole to greet us.

"There's Ms. Terry," Dilys said. Ms. Terry was the nicest of the sixth-grade teachers. We were lucky to get in her class.

Four more buses pulled in behind ours. The doors opened and sixth-graders spilled out. Then we were herded into the building. I grabbed Dilys' arm, half afraid, half excited.

Inside the lobby, everyone milled around in confused bunches.

"Wow. This place looks like a mall," I remarked, awestruck.

"Are you kidding? It looks like Epcot Center," Dilys put in.

I had never been to Epcot Center, so I'd have to take her word for it. The ceiling of the lobby went up and up and *up*, three open stories. From where we stood, we could see the second and third floors miles above our heads.

One of the teachers, not ours, yelled to get our attention. I figured she was the head teacher.

"Students, quiet, please! Classes are in session. Sound carries in the atrium. I want to welcome you to your new school. I'm sure you are as excited as we are to be in such a wonderful facility. Our classrooms are located on the second floor. As we go down the hall and up the stairs, remember to keep your voices *down*. We are here as guests, and we must be on our best behavior. If we abuse our privileges here, we will be sent back to Willow

Springs to stay in trailers. And we don't want that to happen, do we?"

"Suits me," a voice behind me said carelessly.

I turned to see a boy with auburn hair and a chipped front tooth. I recognized Benjamin Potter from fifth grade. He had grown a lot over the summer, put on weight, too, but he was still cute.

Benjamin gave me a grin. "Hey, Maxie. You in Terry's class, too?"

"Yeah. So's Dilys. I'm really nervous about this year," I admitted. "I wish we were back at Willow Springs."

"I don't. Hey, wouldn't it be neat if they couldn't find our names or something? And we didn't go to either school? We could just skip the whole sixth grade."

"But they've already got our names," I pointed out logically. "We all got letters."

"I can dream, can't I?"

In two single-file lines we started down the long hall. I felt good with Dilys in front of me and Benjamin Potter behind me. Maybe this year wouldn't be so bad, after all.

Just then a bell rang. Suddenly the halls exploded with big kids, laughing, shouting, screaming at the top of their lungs. Locker doors slammed like gunshots. The high school kids practically mowed us down until a man came out of a glass-windowed office and yelled at them. Dilys and I pressed against the wall to avoid being trampled. Then another bell rang and the hall miraculously emptied, like water running down a drain.

"Lesson Number One," Ms. Terry said, counting heads to make sure we were all still in one piece. "Stay out of the way when the bell rings!"

We walked about a mile down the hall to the stairs. At the top of the stairs, the head teacher stopped us again to issue another dire warning. Instead of railings around the open part, there was a half-wall made of glass blocks. I looked over the wall. The ground floor was a long, long way down.

Benjamin pretended to pitch a baseball over the side. Some other kids had the same idea.

"Get back from there," the head teacher ordered. "Never lean over that wall at any time. Is that clear? Nor are you to throw anything over the wall. If you are caught throwing an object, even a piece of paper, it's an automatic suspension. That's not my rule. It applies to everyone in this school, as a safety precaution."

"Fortress," I muttered.

"What?" said Dilys.

"This place is more like a fortress than a castle."

"You can say that again." Benjamin put his hands in his pockets.

Ms. Terry showed us our lockers. They were orange, a color I hated. The lockers on the first

20

floor were yellow. A bank of free-standing lockers in the middle of the hall were reserved for the sophomores, she informed us. We had the smaller, double-decker lockers built into the wall. Naturally, the high school kids kept the good lockers for themselves. I hoped I wouldn't be assigned a locker on top. I'd never reach.

Ms. Terry stopped at the door of a classroom and waited until the stragglers caught up. "My class, in here, please."

It looked like an ordinary classroom, with desks and chairs and a blackboard. Posters of the Eiffel Tower and Paris decorated one wall. Then I noticed there weren't any windows. None. I didn't like being stuck in a room without any windows at all. It was like being closed in a box. How would we be able to tell it was raining outside, or snowing? How would we know it was still daytime?

"This is normally a French classroom," Ms. Terry explained. "But we can fix it up anyway we like."

"Can we bring in a popcorn machine?" Benjamin Potter asked. "I like a little snack in the afternoon."

I giggled. Ms. Terry merely smiled and told him to take a seat. She didn't even get mad when Benjamin asked her where she wanted him to take it.

Dilys rolled her eyes. "Some things never change."

We picked seats together near the back. "I think he's cute," I said, following Dilys.

"You would."

I twisted around to see who else was from last year's class. "You, me, Benjamin Potter, Michael . . ." I was glad to see some familiar faces. Everyone but me had grown over the summer. I was still the shortest kid in class.

"Katherine, Michelle, Horst the Brain . . ." Dilys added.

"And Ellen."

"Who?" Dilys squinted as if she needed glasses.

I pointed to a blonde girl two desks over. No one claimed the seats around her. She looked like a rock in a stream, sitting alone like that.

"I don't remember her last name," I said.

Ellen was one of those kids who blend in with the woodwork. Observing Ellen hunched over her desk, I realized I had barely escaped Ellen's fate myself. Practically my only outstanding feature so far was speaking clearly. If I wasn't best friends with someone as neat as Dilys Freeman, you wouldn't be able to tell me from the woodwork, either.

Ms. Terry called roll, then sat on the edge of her desk to tell us what our year would be like. She wore a long skirt of silky material and sandals with straps that tied around her ankles. I knew I was going to love her.

"Room 228 is our new home for the year, but we won't be in this classroom all the time," she began. "You will share the cafeteria, the gym, and the playing fields outside with the high school students. We have been given permission to use some of the other facilities here, as well."

Next Ms. Terry assigned lockers. My heart dropped two stories. I was given one of the top lockers. Dilys had the one below mine. We filed out into the hall to practice opening them.

"Want to switch?" Dilys offered when she saw me struggling to reach the combination lock.

"If you don't mind," I said gratefully. Dilys handed me the paper with the combination on it and took mine. I bent down eye-level with the combination dial. It looked like a safe and was about as hard to get into. I had trouble opening the front door at home with a key! How would I ever get the hang of a combination lock?

Dilys spun her dial expertly and clicked open her locker. I rocked back on my heels, filled with dismay. As far back as fourth grade, I worried about having to open a locker. Todd started junior high that year, and he made it sound like a terrible ordeal. I wasn't supposed to face lockers until I got to seventh grade, but I had to do it *now*, a whole year ahead of schedule!

"Here." Dilys shut her own locker. "Let me show you."

I felt like the dumbest person in the world. I hadn't been in high school an hour and already I was flunking out!

Back in room 228, Ms. Terry issued spelling and math books. The rest of our textbooks would be sent over from Willow Springs Elementary by the end of the week. A student from one of the other sixth-grade classes came to the door to hand Ms. Terry a note.

"We have an all-school assembly at Willow Springs," she read out loud. "Today, at two o'clock. The buses will be out front at one forty-five to take us over."

Dilys made the high sign. Today would be a short day!

Bells rang all morning. Though none of the high school kids came down our hall, we could hear them stamping overhead like a herd of water buffalo. I wondered how we would learn anything with all the noise.

Ms. Terry prepared us for the lunch drill.

"The sixth-graders are scheduled to have lunch on the B shift," she told us. "B shift begins at eleven-thirty, but we'll go down five minutes early. That way, you'll have a head start in the serving line. We have a special table reserved for us, so you won't have to scramble for seats."

At twenty-five after eleven, we marched down-stairs. The cafeteria was located across from the atrium. An electronic board above the double doors flashed messages: "Happy Birthday, Debbie, From the Gang"; "The Latin Club will meet on Tuesdays at 3:30"; "Go Wildcats!"

A wildcat, the school mascot, was painted on the wall next to the cafeteria. Bands of blue and white, Centreville's colors, framed the snarling cat.

The cafeteria seemed bigger than our whole elementary school. There were three hot-food lines and a salad bar in the center of the room. We maneuvered around a sea of tables and chairs to get in line. High school food, I soon learned, didn't look any better than elementary school food.

"I'm bringing my lunch from now on," I said to Dilys, taking a plate of limp nachos. "Even peanut butter is better than this stuff."

"I know! Let's bring lunch for each other. You bring for both of us tomorrow and I'll bring for us the next day."

Leave it to Dilys to come up with a brilliant solution. "A picnic every day! Great idea. I'll bring tuna sandwiches tomorrow."

"No onions, lots of mayo on mine." Dilys led the way to the long table reserved for the sixth-grad-ers.

Just then the double doors were flung open and

a boiling mass of high school kids thundered into the cafeteria. I nearly dropped my tray. The big kids seethed around the tables, cutting us off from the path we were taking to our table.

"No fair," an older boy griped to his friend as they pushed past us to the serving line. "The Munchkins get to eat before we do."

I turned to Dilys, still gripping my tray. "Munchkins?"

"I think they mean us," she replied sourly. "Look, there's your brother."

Todd started past us with some guys I didn't recognize. Gary and Boris, Todd's skateboard cronies, must have another lunch shift.

Balancing my tray on one hand, I plucked at his Hawaiian shirt. "Hi!"

"Hi, Todd!" Dilys chimed.

He looked at us, then glanced away quickly. He didn't smile or say hi back. A tiny muscle worked in his jaw. I wondered what was bugging him. I soon found out.

"Hey, Granville, I didn't know your girlfriends were so young," a guy with blond spikes jeered.

"Talk about robbing the cradle!"

"Rock-a-bye, baby!"

Todd's blue eyes darkened. "Lay off, you guys. That's just my stupid sister."

"Stupid sister! Oh, yeah?" I said indignantly. "That makes you *my* stupid brother!"

One of his friends reached out and patted Dilys on the head, like a dog. "Good little Munchkin. Go have your cookies and milk."

Todd patted me, too. "Run along, now, kiddies."

The boys left, laughing.

I was so insulted, I couldn't speak. I stared at Todd's flamingo-printed back, wanting to murder him. How dare he humiliate me in the middle of the cafeteria! As Dilys and I headed for our table once again, a girl patted us on the head the same way Todd and his friend did.

"The freshmen are getting smaller every year," she said to the guy she was with.

"I can't believe they let infants in our school," the boy remarked. "What do they think this is, a day-care center? We ought to rename the place Munchkinland." They moved on.

"The next person who pats me on the head is going to get it on the shins," Dilys said angrily.

"Where do they get off, calling us Munchkins?" I was furious. I didn't want to be in their dumb old school any more than they wanted us here, but at least they could treat us like human beings. And Todd! Since when did he get so high and mighty he couldn't say hello to his own sister!

After lunch, we trooped back upstairs to room 228. Because we were going to an assembly later, we skipped recess. I didn't think that was fair, either. At least Ms. Terry didn't make us work. She read us two chapters from a book called *Johnny Tremain*. At last it was time to catch the bus to Willow Springs Elementary.

I was glad to leave Centreville. I missed my old school. At least there we were appreciated!

As the bus jounced along, I imagined the lower grades greeting us with banners and a brass band, to welcome back the returning heroes. After all, we had survived one day at Centreville High and that was worth a balloon launch, at least.

But no marching band or cheering crowd met us at the door. Instead we were hustled down the hall like people entering a theater after the play has started. In the gym, the other classes were already seated on the bleachers. The principal, Mr. Rice, spoke into the microphone.

"Here they are. Please take your seats quickly, sixth-graders," the principal said, rather impatiently. "We have a great program and we don't want to run out of time."

The only seats left were way at the top. We had to climb over little kids to reach the top rows.

"Who are they?" a little girl asked her friend.

"Sixth-graders," the other girl replied, not budging so I was forced to step over her. "They think they're so smart."

A boy commented in a snobby tone, "Why don't

they go back where they came from? We don't want them."

Some heroic welcome! I thought, taking my seat at the very top of the bleachers. We had only been away from this school one day, not even a *whole* day, and the little kids couldn't remember who we were!

A first-grader stepped up to the microphone and began singing the school song in a small voice. The principal urged us to join in. Most of the students didn't know the words.

We sixth-graders knew the song by heart. I looked around. Only a few sixth-graders were singing. Benjamin Potter sat with his lips buttoned shut. So did Dilys and Katherine and Michelle. I didn't blame them. After that welcome home, who felt like singing?

The scene reminded me of a movie I'd seen once about a man who wasn't allowed to stay in any country. He had to sail on the ocean all the time. He couldn't live on dry land because he didn't belong anywhere.

We were like the man without a country. We didn't belong at Willow Springs anymore. And we certainly didn't belong at Centreville High.

We were sixth-graders without a school.

3

"People are a lot like animals . . . or is it the other way around?"
— *Maxie Granville's Theory of Life*, Vol. II

It's sort of a fad," I complained to my mother, who was listening with half an ear as she went over yesterday's sales figures for The Rabbit Hole. "The kids pat us on the head like we're dogs or something. I hate it."

"Maybe you ought to snap at them," Mom teased. "Snarl the next time somebody does it."

"Mo-om! This is serious!"

She looked up from her papers. "Sorry, dear. I don't think it is. The older kids are annoying you now, but they'll get bored and quit after a while."

"They haven't so far, and it's been two weeks, almost."

"Well, sixth-graders in their school is still a novelty."

Who's side was she on? "Novelty! They act like

we're from another *planet*." I pushed aside a stack of picture books to make room for my after-school microwave pizza. I was starving. Today was Dilys' turn to bring lunch. I nearly passed out when she unwrapped three thick, sloppy liverwurst sandwiches. Liverwurst! With horseradish! I forgot about Dilys' nonconformist tastes in food.

My mother frowned over her receipts, never noticing I had fixed an entire pizza before supper. She'd been that way ever since she started the bookstore. My mother used to have a job as a secretary in a private school. But then she and her friend Lola, a teacher at the same school, decided to open a bookstore for children.

They called the shop The Rabbit Hole, after *Alice's Adventures in Wonderland*. Dad joked that we'd all be in the poorhouse if the store didn't succeed. I didn't think it was very funny, but Dad remarked he'd rather pour his money down a rabbit hole than hand it over to the government. Bankruptcy hardly sounded like a barrel of fun, but were my parents worried?

All summer Mom was frantic about the name of the shop, the location, the size of their inventory, whether they could get famous authors and illustrators to visit and sign books . . . everything but money! Why my mother ever gave up her nice regular job typing letters is beyond me.

One good thing about the store was that Mom

was often home when I got home from school. She traded closing the shop for doing the daily bookkeeping.

Just then she glanced up from her figures, as if what I'd been saying all along had finally sunk in. "Todd doesn't do that, does he? Pat you on the head like a dog?"

"Not since the first day." Todd and I had made an agreement. He wouldn't give me Munchkin pats, and I would never, ever speak to him or act like I knew him in school.

"That's good," Mom said, satisfied. "You'll settle into a routine. Soon high school will be old hat."

Actually we *had* settled into sort of a routine, but high school would never be "old hat." Not in a thousand years.

Before she unlocked her own locker, Dilys automatically opened mine. "What would you do without me?" she said.

"Carry my books around all day, I guess," I tossed back lightly. It wasn't funny, really. Everyone had adjusted to the move but me.

Most of the kids in our class acted like it wasn't any big deal to be going to Centreville, especially Katherine and Michelle. They were both twelve and talked about boys and clothes all the time, like the high school girls.

"ESC today," Dilys said, handing me my science book.

"Good." I cheered up immediately.

The Environmental Science Center, called ESC for short, was an oasis in the desert of high school life.

Our second day at Centreville, Ms. Terry gave us the grand tour. We saw the Media Center — a fancy name for the glass-walled library on the ground floor — the writing labs, the photography darkrooms, and the television studio. We wouldn't be allowed to use any of those rooms.

In the home-ec department, some tenth-grade girls offered us oatmeal cookies warm from the oven. Benjamin Potter gagged like he was being poisoned. Ms. Terry made him stand out in the hall while we finished touring the first floor. The second floor just had classrooms, including the Willow Springs Annex.

Upstairs on the third floor, we were shown the biology and chemistry labs, which looked like a lot of sinks to me. Then Ms. Terry opened the door of the ESC.

"We will be using this facility," she told us, "two days a week, to learn about science."

The ESC was like a pet store and a greenhouse rolled into one. In bubbling aquariums, colorful fish darted among rocks and seashells. Shelves of potted plants and flowers grew under purple lights. Along one wall there were empty cages that would be filled, Ms. Terry said, with different animals and insects throughout the year. A pink-eyed white rabbit named Garcia made his home in a hutch near the wide windows.

Today I clock-watched until it was time for science. When we were settled in the ESC, Ms. Terry asked, "Who would like to feed Garcia?" The sixth-graders had been given the responsibility of taking care of the bunny.

"Me! Me!" Benjamin Potter boomed. He waved his hand so wildly he practically fell out of his chair.

Ms. Terry pointed to me. "Maxie and . . . Ellen."

Ellen Dietzler got up, pushing her pale silky hair behind her ears. Her cheeks glowed with pleasure. Teachers hardly ever called on Ellen to do things. I think they forgot she was there. But Ms. Terry seemed to be making a special effort to include Ellen.

In her rush to the back of the room where Garcia's hutch was, Ellen accidentally brushed against Benjamin's desk.

"Sorry," she mumbled, reaching out to keep Benjamin's books from sliding to the floor.

"You're sorry-*looking*," Benjamin cracked.

Michael piped up. "Benjy's got a girlfriend! Benjy's got a girlfriend!"

Benjamin's face turned the color of an eggplant. "Shut up!" he growled. "I wouldn't touch that stupid girl if she was the last girl on earth. She's slimy!"

Flushed with embarrassment, Ellen scooped dry rabbit food from the bag in the cupboard. I got some lettuce leaves and a carrot from the little refrigerator built into the counter.

"You want to give him the carrot?" I said to Ellen. Garcia nibbled his carrot in a cute way.

"No, you go ahead," Ellen said shyly.

After feeding the rabbit, I went back to my seat. Benjamin sprayed me with an imaginary hose.

"De-slime! You came in contact with Slimeball Dietzler."

I laughed. But then I looked over at Ellen and was sorry I did. She pretended to be reading her science book, but her neck was stiff. Too stiff. She'd heard him, too.

I wondered why I'd laughed. Benjamin Potter wasn't that funny. Last year he was cute, but this year he was a loud-mouthed show-off. He said things that made people uncomfortable.

"Ellen reminds me of that rabbit," Dilys said.

"She does? How?"

"Well, she just kind of sits there and doesn't say much. She even looks a little like him."

I giggled. Ellen *did* have white-blonde hair and pale blue eyes. "Maybe she eats lettuce and carrots, too."

Dilys shrugged, already losing interest. She never stayed on any subject too long. "Who knows?"

Ms. Terry gave us our science assignment. "I'd like you to write a paragraph about an animal. There are books in the back you may use. Choose any animal. When you're finished, we'll read our paragraphs in class."

"Can we write about a warthog?" Benjamin, naturally.

"Any animal," Ms. Terry repeated.

"How about a dead animal? I saw this squirrel on the road on the way to school today. It was all — "

"Benjamin." Ms. Terry went on. "When you've picked your animal, I'll write it on the board so we don't have duplicates."

There was a mad dash for the bookcase at the back of the room. Only Dilys remained in her seat.

"Ms. Terry, I already know what I'm going to write about: the duckbill platypus."

The teacher wrote *duckbill platypus* next to Dilys' name. Leave it to Dilys to pick an animal nobody had ever heard of. Soon the others began

36

calling out their choices. I thought about doing my paragraph on rabbits, but Ellen shyly claimed that topic first. Then I thought about doing my report on cats, but Katherine beat me to it. Michelle chose bears. Desperately I leafed through the books. All the good animals were being taken.

When the board was filled with names, Ms. Terry said, "Does everyone have a topic?"

"I don't," I said, feeling dumber than ever. How hard was it to pick an animal? There were thousands of animals, yet none of them appealed to me.

Ms. Terry skimmed the list on the board. "We've covered all the big animals. And we have plenty of rodents."

"I'll say," Benjamin put in.

"Maxie, why don't you do your report on the mole? Now there's an interesting animal."

Moles! I couldn't believe I agreed to such a stupid topic.

Michelle and Katherine snickered. Benjamin made woofing noises. He thought he sounded like a mole. I slunk back to my seat and got out my school notebook. Inside the back flap was a green spiral notebook, my *Theory of Life*, Vol. II. I took it with me to school in case I discovered a new theory about life. Dilys was jotting notes from the encyclopedia opened on her desk. Sighing, I got busy, too.

My book only had two pages on moles. As I read, I learned the mole wasn't such a dumb animal after all. Moles are very industrious. They dig tunnels and eat grubs and go about their business. A realistic, no-nonsense animal.

When it was time to read our paragraphs, Dilys volunteered first. The duckbill platypus, she explained, was a strange animal that laid eggs and carried its babies in a pouch. Ms. Terry let Benjamin Potter go next, obviously to get his turn over with. In a loud voice he told us about warthogs. He would have stayed up in front of the class all day, snorting like a warthog, but Ms. Terry made him sit down.

When there were no more volunteers, Ms. Terry called on us at random. Ellen whispered her report about rabbits. Then it was Michael's turn to tell us about great white sharks. Katherine went next and Michelle followed her. At last it was my turn.

I was halfway through reading my paragraph when a new theory of life hit me. I couldn't wait to write it down. Everybody picked an animal that suited their personality! Dilys wrote about a weird animal. Benjamin did his report on the warthog, which he resembled more every day. Michael wasn't mean like a shark but he was the best swimmer at our pool. Michelle was cute, like the bear cub she picked. Katherine seemed very catlike. Ellen was more like a rabbit than Garcia.

And me? I suppose I had a lot in common with moles. We're both neat and clean . . . and not very exciting.

Downstairs in room 228, Ms. Terry reminded us of a spelling test that Friday. "Let's break into pairs so you have someone to study with."

The room erupted with the sound of scraping desks. Michelle moved her chair next to Katherine's. Benjamin yelled for Michael to come on over. I started to slide my chair next to Dilys — Dilys is not the type to move *her* desk — when Ms. Terry held up a hand.

"No, not your friends this time. I'll assign partners."

She paired Michelle with Bryan and Katherine with Michael. Benjamin got Ellen for a partner. Dilys was Alison's partner, and I was assigned to work with Horst, the class "genius." Horst could probably outspell the dictionary.

Suddenly a book slammed on the floor. Benjamin Potter stood up.

"Benjamin." Ms. Terry frowned. "What is this commotion?"

"I'm not sitting with *her*." He made an obnoxious noise at Ellen.

Ellen ducked her head, her expression hidden beneath a curtain of silky hair.

Ms. Terry marched over to Benjamin's desk. "Benjamin, sentences instead of recess today. You will not speak rudely in this class. How do you think Ellen feels?"

"I don't care how she feels. I'm not sitting next to her. I'll get slimed." He crossed his arms, standing his ground.

Michael snickered.

Ms. Terry was a nice teacher, but she didn't put up with outright disobedience. "Michael, do you want to stay in and write sentences along with Benjamin?" To Benjamin she warned, "One more rude comment and you'll go to Mr. Rice's office." The principal was back at Willow Springs, but kids could still be sent over by car. "Now move your chair over to Ellen's desk. I'll be watching you."

With great reluctance and a lot of unnecessary scraping, Benjamin dragged his chair over to Ellen's desk. He placed it as far out in the aisle as he could. When Ellen handed him the spelling list, he picked it up with the tips of two fingers, as if he didn't want to get contaminated.

"He is *so* immature," Dilys murmured as I steered my chair past. "He acts like an elementary school kid."

"He *is* an elementary school kid," I said. "We all are."

"You don't have to *act* like one," Dilys argued. "Time to grow up. Be mature."

"Like you?"

"Like me."

I studied Dilys to see what a mature eleven-year-old looked like. Today she wore a long denim skirt five sizes too big, probably a tag-sale bargain, and a tie-dyed T-shirt. With her sandals she had on saggy white socks. I wondered if all non-conformists dressed like goatherders.

"Maxie," Ms. Terry warned, her good mood worn down by Benjamin's misbehavior. "You're wasting time."

As I pushed my chair to the front of the room where Horst sat, I felt someone staring at me. I turned around, expecting Dilys to be waving at me. But Dilys was busy with her spelling partner. Ellen Dietzler was watching me, though. Our eyes locked for a second. Then I looked away and hurried to the front of the room before Horst started without me.

It was Dilys' turn to bring our lunch again. We sat down at the sixth-grade table while the other kids got in the serving line. Dilys pulled a series of plastic containers out of the grocery bag she'd brought our lunch in.

"What *is* this stuff?" I asked, opening one of the boxes. Something brown and not very appetizing stared up at me.

"Mushroom caps." Dilys flipped open the other

boxes. "This is sausage quiche and this is pasta salad. My mom had people over last night. I brought the leftovers."

Cold sausage quiche was not my idea of lunch. Neither was liverwurst. Would Dilys ever bring any normal food, like a plain old ham-and-cheese sandwich? She never asked me what I wanted. But when I asked her what *she* wanted, she was quick to put in her order.

Katherine and Michelle sat down next to me. I noticed an empty chair beside Katherine, but I didn't pay much attention to it. Michelle's lunch looked so good I was wondering if she'd trade a mushroom cap for a french fry. Maybe if I sweetened the deal with a quarter.

The bell shrilled, and high school kids swarmed into the cafeteria like an army of fire ants. Without our five-minute head start, we'd never get a crumb.

Ellen Dietzler was the last sixth-grader to get her lunch tray. She was always last because no one ever let her cut in line or gave her backsies. She weaved between the big kids, aiming for the empty chair beside Katherine.

Katherine saw her coming and immediately put her purse on the chair. "This seat is saved," she told Ellen. "You can't sit here."

Ellen knew she was the very last person

through the food line. Everyone else had already found a seat. "Who's it saved for?" she asked.

"My purse!" Katherine quipped, giggling.

Michelle laughed and I did, too, even though I didn't think it was all that funny. I felt a little queasy but blamed it on the mushroom caps.

Ellen finally left to sit in the empty chair beside the teachers, the chair reserved for troublemakers.

"She gives me the creeps," Katherine remarked, staring at the back of Ellen's head.

"Me, too," Michelle agreed. "I don't blame Benjamin for not wanting to sit with her. *I* wouldn't want to be stuck with her."

"Me, either," chimed in a third voice. The voice belonged to me. I'd never considered that sitting next to Ellen Dietzler would be such a disaster, but I hated to be the only dissenting vote at the table.

"What about you?" I asked Dilys.

"What about me?" she said.

Katherine and Michelle started talking about a TV show. They weren't paying attention to our conversation anymore, but I still wanted to know how Dilys felt about Ellen.

"Would you sit next to Ellen Dietzler?"

"I don't sit next to anybody. They sit next to *me*." A typical Dilys answer. "Actually," she went on. "I wish I didn't have to sit with anybody here. It's such a drag, having to sit at our own special table, like little kids." Her gray eyes met mine. "Oh, Maxie, you know I don't mean you. I meant them." With a jerk of her head, she indicated Katherine and Michelle.

I wasn't reassured. If Dilys was bored with Katherine and Michelle, she was probably getting bored with me, too. After all, what was exciting about Maxie the mole?

4

"People are like animals . . . only animals don't change."
— *Maxie Granville's Theory of Life*, Vol. II

Monday morning, I overslept. In my hurry to catch the bus, I didn't see Todd's skateboard in the hall. My foot hooked the board and I went flying. The carpeting cushioned my fall but burned my knees.

"Todd!" I screamed, even though I knew he wasn't there. Todd's classes started at eight. By the time the sixth-grade buses rolled up in front of Centreville High, the older kids were starting second period. My brother got up an hour earlier than I did — early enough to set boobytraps for his sister.

Mom heard the bump and rushed out from the kitchen. "Are you all right?"

"Yes . . . I think. Todd left that thing in the way," I said, close to tears. "I nearly broke my neck."

"He was going to take it to school, but he changed his mind," Mom commented, rolling the offending skateboard into Todd's hogpen of a bedroom.

I rubbed my sore knees. "Take his skateboard to school? What for? Does he have Freshman Skateboard?"

"I think he was planning to skateboard after school in the parking lot with Gary and Boris. But then he called Gary and changed his mind. He seemed kind of upset."

"That's no reason to leave his stupid skateboard in the hall," I said angrily. I was really late now. I wouldn't have time for breakfast.

"You're right," Mom agreed, handing me a muffin to munch at the bus stop. "I'll speak to him this afternoon. I'm worried about him, though. He's having trouble adjusting to high school."

"Worried about *him*? What about me?"

"What about you?"

"Aren't you worried about me making the adjustment? I'm going to high school, too, you know." I shrugged into my sweater, the muffin clamped between my teeth.

"Yes, honey, but it's different for you. Your class is isolated in a separate wing. You're still a sixth-grader. Todd truly belongs in high school. It's important for him to get into the spirit of things."

Mom picked up a pile of papers Todd had left on the table by the door. A flyer on top announced a door-decorating contest sponsored by SADD. I didn't know what SADD stood for but it certainly described the mood I was in.

I just barely made the bus. Dilys, who snitched half of my muffin, headed for our favorite seat in the back. I followed, as always. Today the bus seemed crowded with rowdier-than-usual kids. Two more stops and the lower grades would get off at Willow Springs Elementary, leaving the sixth-graders to go on to Centreville High.

Dilys wasn't in a very good mood, either. "I hate riding with all these little kids," she grumbled, wrinkling her nose at a couple of fourth-graders who were fighting right next to us.

"Too bad we don't have a private limo," I said, ready to unload my own complaints about my brother. Dilys was lucky — her brother lived with their father.

The bus driver yelled for everyone in the back-seat to behave, which made us mad because we weren't doing anything.

"See? They lump us all together. And we aren't like them anymore." Dilys pulled a sheet of paper from her flowered tote bag. "Look what I found."

The paper was covered with footprints, but I recognized it as the flyer for the door-decorating

47

contest. "Todd has one of those," I said. "What is SADD?"

Dilys smoothed the crumpled sheet. "It's a group. Students Against Drunk Driving. Kids decorate their homeroom doors, and the winner donates the money they win to the local chapter of SADD. You sign up your homeroom here."

"Todd is probably supposed to sign up his homeroom. But I guess he had better things to do, like sabotage his sister. I suppose that's why he brought the form home. So what?"

Dilys stared at me. "So what? Didn't you hear me? Only *homerooms* can enter the contest. We don't have a homeroom. They're deliberately leaving us out and it's not fair. I'm going to protest."

The bus stopped to unload the kids at Willow Springs. In all the yelling and confusion, I didn't understand Dilys' last sentence. "You're going to what?" I asked.

"Protest. They can't do this to us. We should be allowed to enter that contest."

"But, Dilys, it's for high school kids!"

"What's that got to do with the price of tea in China?" Her eyes were very dark, that stormy color that meant trouble.

"We're not in high school, Dilys. We just *go* to high school. We're still basically sixth-graders," I said, parroting my mother. "They can have their contest and leave us out if they want to. It's their school."

"And you don't mind being ignored? Except when they pick on us?"

I did mind. I hated being treated like a boarder, as Todd called us. I hated Munchkin Pats. But I didn't see how protesting a high school contest would change things, and said as much.

"You wait," Dilys said staunchly. "I'll show you."

Before Ms. Terry could begin our first lesson, Dilys brought up the contest.

"It says here the entire school can enter, but there's only a place for homerooms to sign up," she concluded, giving Ms. Terry the crumpled entry form. "I think we should be in the contest, too. We don't have a homeroom but we have doors."

Ms. Terry studied the flyer. "You're right, Dilys. The rules imply that only students with homerooms may enter the contest. You obviously feel strongly about this. How many others believe the sixth-graders should be allowed to enter the contest? How many of you agree with Dilys? Let's see hands."

A forest of hands waved in the air. I raised mine, too, even though I wasn't sure what point Dilys was trying to make. Did she want the sixth graders to be a part of this school or was she only interested in the contest? I bet the other kids didn't know, either, but they raised their hands just to put off doing math a little longer.

Ms. Terry took the situation seriously. "I'll bring up the matter to Ms. Johnson at lunch," she said, referring to the sixth-grade teacher who'd welcomed us on the first day at Centreville High. "If the other classes feel the same, we have a case to present to the principal here."

Dilys' popularity skyrocketed at lunch. Katherine and Michelle fought to sit next to her, barely leaving room for me, her best friend. Benjamin Potter even gave Dilys a slightly used cupcake from his lunch.

"It's a little smooshed," he explained. "I didn't bite it or anything. Hey, Dil, if this contest thing works, see what you can do to get us out of math."

"I can't help it you don't study," Dilys said, but she took the cupcake and gave the bottom half to me, saving the icing half for herself. I could tell she was feeling pretty good.

By the end of the day, the Centreville High principal agreed that the nine sixth-grade classes could enter the contest. Where it said "homeroom" on the entry form, we were supposed to write in our room number. The doors would be judged Friday afternoon.

When Ms. Terry made the announcement, our

windowless walls rang with cheers. Dilys stood up and bowed. I applauded along with the others, but the whole time I wondered about Dilys. She would never have bowed a year ago. Back in fifth grade, when our teacher asked us to give Horst a hand because he got the highest score on a test, Dilys would look at me and clap with two index fingers. She hated kids who grabbed all the attention.

Now *she* was the center of attention, and her head seemed to swell with the glory. Especially when the class elected Dilys the chief door-decorator. I figured kids would mob her at recess, wanting to be on her committee.

On nice days, we had recess outside on a black-top area set aside for sixth-graders. If the weather was rotten, we had to squeeze into the small gym and play quiet games. Outside, we could play whatever we wanted. But today nobody wanted to play anything. All the kids clamored around Dilys, begging to be on her committee.

"I only need three people," Dilys said. "Katherine . . ." Katherine squealed as if she'd just been chosen Miss America. ". . . Michael . . . and . . . hmmmmm, let's see."

"Me! Me!"

I stood back from the circle. I didn't have to beg. Dilys was going to pick me, wasn't she?

"Somebody good in art," Dilys was saying. Her

gaze passed right over me and lit on Alison Mosconi. "Alison. Okay, that's it. Katherine, Michael, and Alison. Come over here, guys. We've got to talk."

The losers groaned in disappointment, drifting off to start up games. I turned away from Dilys, stunned. She didn't pick me. Her very own best friend!

At the edge of the blacktop, apart from the others, Ellen Dietzler watched me. She hadn't begged to be on Dilys' committee. Nobody ever picked her to do anything. She was always left out of games unless Ms. Terry forced a team to take her. She looked like she felt sorry for me. The last thing I wanted was her pity.

With a final glance at Dilys, I stalked over to Michelle's game of four-square. She needed a fourth player, but I didn't suggest Ellen. I was too upset with my best friend to worry about the class outcast.

After recess, Ms. Terry excused Dilys and her committee from history. They pulled their chairs into the corner and talked softly, laughing every so often, while the rest of us slogged through the War of 1812. I didn't have a chance to speak to Dilys until it was time to go home. Not that I wanted to.

Dilys dragged her chair back to her desk, telling Katherine she would call her tonight. As she stuffed books and papers into her tote bag, she must have suddenly remembered my existence in the world.

"You're mad," she stated.

"I'm not mad," I lied.

"You are, too. You're mad because I didn't ask you to be on the door committee." Pushing her bangs back, she sighed. "Maxie, you know I would have picked you, but this door contest is very important. I need people who are — "

"Good in art," I finished sourly. "Don't bother explaining, Dilys."

"Maxie, do you remember the transportation project last year?"

How could I forget? Dilys was my partner. We had to make a model showing a form of transportation. Dilys wanted to build a covered wagon, but I said it was too hard. Finally we settled on an Ohio flatboat. We were supposed to build it together, but Dilys only let me glue Popsicle sticks to the bottom of the boat after I messed up the pilot's cabin. We got an A on the project, no thanks to me, as Dilys said afterward.

But that wasn't any reason to leave me off her committee. The door contest wasn't going to be graded. We were friends and friends stuck together. *True* friends, that is.

"Maxie — " Dilys began, but I stood up, ready for Ms. Terry's signal. High school dismissed an hour earlier, so there weren't any bells after two-thirty. Instead, our teacher dismissed us when it was time to go home.

The instant Ms. Terry said we could leave, I raced down the hall, aiming to be first on the bus. I sat down next to a kid from one of the other sixth-grade classes. Now I wouldn't have to sit with Dilys and listen to her drone on and on about the stupid contest.

There were important things in *my* life, too.

If only I knew what they were.

The theme of the contest was "Protect Your Dream." Friday, as we walked through the halls to the cafeteria and, later, to recess, I saw some of the entries. One door had a construction-paper car wrecked against a tree. Another door showed a martini glass with a set of car keys floating in it. Those doors clearly said it was wrong to drink and drive, but they didn't have much to do with dreams, I thought.

Dilys and her committee worked on our door through lunch. First they draped the whole door with pale blue construction paper and then covered it with plastic film swirled with all the colors of the rainbow. Michael drew a fancy sports car with the top down. You could see the back of the person driving it but you couldn't tell if it was a boy or a girl. Katherine and Alison glued cottonball clouds to the plastic film and then taped the car just below the clouds. Dilys added the final touch, white wings attached to the doors of the car, so it looked like the car was flying into the clouds.

"Looks neat," I told her grudgingly. It *was* a terrific door.

"Thanks. It's pretty good, but there are a lot of really great doors," she replied, gnawing a thumbnail.

We waited on pins and needles for the judges to come around. We must have been last on their list because it was nearly one-thirty before they showed up. The judges examined our door a long time, making notes on a clipboard. Dilys clutched her science book with white knuckles. Even though I was still mad at her, I hoped our door would win.

At two-twenty, the principal's voice came over the loudspeaker with the end-of-the-day announcements. "We are happy to announce the winners of the SADD door-decorating contest," he said. "There were so many terrific entries, it was difficult choosing the top three winners. Third prize goes to room 107. Second prize to room 228, which is in the Willow Springs Annex — "

Cheers drowned out the rest of the principal's words. Benjamin and Michael jumped up and down. We yelled again when an aide from the office hung a red second-place ribbon on our door-knob. Ms. Terry gave up trying to teach science and let us have a free period.

I decided to forgive Dilys for not picking me to be on her committee. Her door earned the sixth-graders well-deserved attention and that was what mattered.

By Monday, it was all over the school that one of the Munchkin rooms had placed in the contest. High school kids cruised down our hall to see the prizewinning door. They weren't supposed to — the Annex was off-limits to the big kids — but they snuck down anyway.

"You're a celebrity," I said to Dilys.

"No, I'm not," she replied as a group of tenth-graders peeked into our classroom. "Our door is. They can't believe the little baby sixth-graders can do anything important. I tried to show them."

At lunch an astonishing thing happened. It was my turn to bring the food. I was setting out egg salad sandwiches when a ninth-grade girl came over to our table. Her hair was as red as fire — obviously dyed.

"Who's the kid who designed that super door?" she demanded.

Katherine pointed to Dilys. "She thought it up. But I helped make the door."

"Really?" The girl stared at Dilys. I noticed she had on a droopy skirt. Her flashing hair looked even messier than Dilys'. They could have been sisters. "What's your name, kid?"

"Dilys. What's yours, *kid*?"

The older girl laughed. "Hey, you're all right! Want to come eat with us?" She pointed to a table nearby. "A bunch of us like to talk about art and stuff. If you're allowed, that is."

Dilys snatched one of my sandwiches. "Sure, we're allowed. We aren't prisoners or anything."

My mouth dropped open. Dilys was leaving the sixth-grade table and going to sit with the ninth-graders! She didn't care if Ms. Terry saw her. Worse, she didn't even say good-bye to me or ask me to come with her. So much for her promise to stick together and not go crazy just because we were in high school. In two seconds, Dilys had broken our pact.

I knew then, with a queasy feeling not helped by the smell of egg salad, that Dilys was sick of hanging around Maxie the mole.

5

"Just when things are as bad as they can be,
they get worse."
    — *Maxie Granville's Theory of Life*, Vol. II

I was still upset when I got home from school. Dilys made a feeble attempt to talk to me on the bus, but I turned my head away. She only tried once. Dilys Freeman was not the type to plead with anyone, not even her best friend.

The house was quiet. A note from Mom under the fake asparagus magnet on the refrigerator said that she'd be coming home later than usual but that Todd would be there to watch me. Watch me! As if I needed watching! Of course she couldn't have said that he'd be home to keep me company because it would have been a big fat lie. Even when there were just the two of us, Todd seldom bothered with me.

But today I didn't hear the familiar whoosh of

skateboard wheels carving patterns in the driveway. I didn't hear the television set or the stereo
or Todd yakking on the phone. Did he leave without waiting for me get home? Todd wouldn't directly disobey one of Mom's orders. If she said to
be here when I got home, he was here . . .
somewhere.

But where? And why was it so quiet?

"Todd?" I said, peeping over the pass-through
counter into the den. I could see the back of Dad's
recliner chair. Then I noticed the tuft of brown
hair poking up over the top.

"Todd, is that you?" What was wrong with him?
Why didn't he answer? Why didn't he *move*? Was
he sick? Hurt? Mom was forever making the dire
prediction that Todd would meet an untimely end
on his skateboard.

I rushed into the den, frantically trying to remember the first aid I'd learned at camp and only
coming up with how long to leave a tourniquet on
a snakebite.

Todd *looked* like he had been bitten by a snake.
Or a tarantula, or something with a poisonous
sting. He was slumped in Dad's chair like an old
teddy bear with half the stuffing missing, his eyes
glazed over, his breathing shallow.

I screamed.

He screamed, too, jerking to life.

"What's wrong with you, scaring me like that" Todd demanded. "Have you lost your mind? Not that you ever had any."

"Me? *You* were the one who scared *me*. What's wrong with *you*, sitting there like that? Why didn't you answer me?"

"I was thinking," he replied.

"So that's what I smelled."

"You wouldn't know what thinking smelled like," he shot back. "It's totally foreign to you."

"I know what burning rubber smells like."

He sneered. "Aren't we smart now that we got to high school?"

That was a low blow. He knew I didn't want to be at Centreville High. He could keep his dumb old school, for all I cared. "You're just jealous," I said airily, "because our class came in second in the door-decorating contest. The ninth-graders didn't even place *last*."

"Second," Todd emphasized, "comes after first. *Way* after first. They just gave it to you little kids so you wouldn't cry, that's why."

"We won fair and square! Our door was good! Did you design your door, Todd? No wonder you lost." I bit my lip, wondering if I'd gone too far. Todd wouldn't beat me up or anything, but he had his own methods of revenge. Once after I tattled on him, he made me drink a glass of pepper water. Another time he put a praying mantis in my bed.

60

But he reacted in a way that was completely unlike crafty old Todd. He flew into a rage.

Jumping up, he grabbed a newspaper from the pile by Dad's chair and flung it at me.

"Don't I have enough troubles!" he railed. "Aren't things bad enough putting up with a bratty little sister at my school? *My* school!"

The whole time he ranted, he tossed newspapers. I quit cowering after the first few and began throwing them back. When he ran out of newspapers he tore pages out of the *TV Guide*. I grabbed some of Mom's magazines and ripped out pages to throw at him. It looked like a paper blizzard.

Todd seized the sofa cushions and pitched them at me. I retaliated with the needlepoint pillows on the loveseat. We were like two crazy people. We just kept throwing things, whatever came into our hands. Surprisingly, we didn't break down laughing. It was as if we were both so angry, we would never get it out of our systems.

"I don't want to be at your stupid school!" I yelled. "I want my own school! I hate it there!"

"So do I!" Todd emptied a bowl of nuts upside down on my head.

I stood there, dazed from the fury of our fight. "You do?" I said unbelievingly. "You hate Centreville, too?"

At that moment, Mom walked in. Her aston-

61

ished gaze took in the trashed den. Our mother was hardly a neatness freak, but she did have a few standards. "If you keep things picked up and neat, the dirt isn't quite as noticeable," she would say.

The den was anything but picked up and neat. Mom gaped at the avalanche of newspapers, pillows, cushions, nuts, magazines, and other stuff we had hurled at each other. Then she said, in a voice that was amazingly calm, "I don't know what went on here and I don't want to know."

"She shot off her mouth — " Todd blurted out.

"He started it — " I said quickly.

Mom interrupted, "I don't care who started it! Pick up every scrap. When I come back in this room, I want to see it spotless, is that understood?" She spun around, heading for her bedroom.

Todd glared at me. "Traitor! Telling Mom I started it!"

"You did!" I said hotly. "If I'm a traitor, then you're a liar!"

We set to work, giving each other wide margins, as if we both had contagious diseases. It took longer to straighten the room than mess it up, but at last the den was back to normal. In fact, the room looked better because we cleaned out Dad's three-week supply of newspapers. Mom failed to see the improvement, though.

When she returned to inspect, she was cool. "I don't know what happened here this afternoon but I'm disappointed in you both. I thought you were old enough to get along, but I guess I was wrong. Since you can't seem to stand the sight of each other, you can go to your rooms until supper."

We went our separate ways, Todd to his room at the end of the hall, me to my room next to the bathroom. Being sent to our rooms wasn't the end of the world, although it was nicer for Todd than for me. He had his own TV and stereo to break the monotony. I had homework, a poor substitute, but better than nothing. I decided to do it early to fill the time.

It was impossible to concentrate on math. I kept thinking about Dilys' desertion at lunch and my fight with Todd. The last thing he said before Mom walked in and caught us was that he hated school, too. Did he hate it so much because I was there?

I hardly ever bumped into Todd, except in the cafeteria. Even then I kept distance according to our agreement. It was hard to pretend I didn't know my own brother, but it seemed to be working okay.

At least I *thought* it was okay. Something triggered Todd's outburst. We'd had our share of fights but nothing like the knock-down-drag-out of this afternoon.

If I cracked my door, I could see the edge of

Todd's door down the hall. I went and looked out.

"Todd?"

He came to his door. "What?"

"I'm sorry about the fight. I just had a bad day today."

"I started it. I should apologize first. I had a crummy day, too." He paused. "I'm sorry I called you a brat. You're not, really."

"And you're not a liar, either," I said. "Todd, I promise I won't even look at you in the cafeteria anymore. I won't embarrass you around your friends."

His sigh nearly blew my door shut. "Don't worry about it, Moondoggie. I don't *have* any friends."

Todd without friends? Ever since I could remember, my brother always had a gang to hang out with. He made friends the first hour we moved to Virginia. He really *must* have had a bad day.

Dilys came over after dinner. I heard her talking to Mom in the kitchen. Mom lifted our sentence, but Todd and I shuffled back to our rooms anyway. I had math to finish. I guess Todd just felt like being alone.

I didn't want to see Dilys, but I had no choice.

" — in her room," I heard Mom telling her. "Go on back, Dilys."

Then I decided that Dilys had come over to

64

apologize. I felt better after I told Todd I was sorry. I suppose I should give my best friend the same chance. But her apology had better be good, delivered on bended knee, and she'd better promise never to leave me like that ever again. . . .

A few seconds later, Dilys walked in.

"Hi," she said, looking fairly conformist in jeans and an old Willow Springs Elementary T-shirt. "What're you doing?"

"Math." I was lying on my stomach on the floor. I didn't get up. Dilys' dirty Nikes were at eye level. I quickly sat up. I wasn't about to stare at anybody's shoes, especially if they were about to apologize to me.

Dilys sat down, cross-legged. She could get up that way, too, with one foot crossed behind the other. Every time I tried it, I toppled over. "The answers are in the back of the book," she said.

"I know. But Ms. Terry wants to see how we got the answer. I still have to work out the problem." I looked at her. "Did you come all the way over here to tell me how I could cheat on my math homework?"

She laughed. "All the way. Maxie, I live two doors over! I don't care if you cheat. If you have the answer, sometimes you can solve the problem by working it backward."

"You can, but not me," I said frostily. "I have enough trouble working it out frontward."

"You're mad at me, aren't you? Because I went with those ninth-graders."

I erased a wrong answer and industriously brushed away the eraser crumbs. "It makes no difference to me where you sit, Dilys Freeman. No difference *whatsoever*."

"See, you are mad." She managed to sound a little irritated, as if I had no right to be mad at her. Dilys often used the ploy of shifting the blame from herself to me when we had a disagreement. Most of the time I let her because it was the only way to keep peace, but this time we hadn't *had* an argument. Dilys broke our pact, plain and simple. I didn't have anything to say about it at all.

She read my stony silence as pouting. "Listen, Maxie, what was I supposed to do? Let that girl think the little sixth-grade baby had to sit with the teacher? Our reputation is at stake here. They liked my door design. They wanted to talk to me. So I sat with them. Big deal."

"You could have taken me."

"They didn't *ask* you. They asked me."

"A *true* friend still would have taken her best friend. Or asked if her friend could sit with them. And if they didn't like it, a *true* friend would have stayed where she was." Not very subtle, but I didn't care. It was time Dilys knew how I felt.

Dilys picked up my pencil and began doodling

on my homework paper. "Let's say I did that, asked the ninth-graders if my friend could come, too. Would you have gone, Maxie? With Ms. Terry watching?"

"Stop messing up my paper." I snatched the pencil away from her. She knew I wouldn't have left the sixth-grade table. We weren't supposed to sit anyplace else, just like we weren't supposed to hang over the half-wall on the second floor or throw things over it.

"Those kids were really interesting," Dilys went on smoothly, already deciding the discussion was over and she had won. "They're into all kinds of neat things. Drama, art, poetry. I can't wait to get to high school and join the drama club."

"What? You mean they didn't skip you ahead three grades? I thought you *were* in high school," I said sarcastically.

Dilys stood up. "There's just no talking to you while you're in this weird mood. Try to get up on the right side of the bed tomorrow, will you?"

I scrambled to a standing position. "No, wait. I'm tired of you walking out and having the last word."

She halted. "Okay. I'm all ears."

Now that I had her undivided attention, I wasn't sure what I wanted to say. "You broke our pact," I accused. "We said we wouldn't change just because we're going to high school, but you have. You even joined the other side. You act like you're one of the big kids now."

"I don't *think* I'm anybody but myself," Dilys returned evenly. "I haven't changed, Maxie. I've matured. There's a difference. But you wouldn't understand. You want everything to be just like it was back in fifth grade."

"I do not!" I denied, even though she was absolutely right.

"Yes, you do. You'd like to be back at Willow Springs with all of the same kids we had in our class last year. I bet you'd be perfectly happy with our old teacher. You'd probably like to memorize the states again and go to Constitution Hall on our field trip. You like everything the same — you're still writing the book we wrote last year."

Close to tears, I kicked the edge of my nightstand to show Dilys her stinging words had no effect on me.

"You can't stay the same," she said. "I don't know why you'd *want* to."

"I hope your new friends let you sit with them every day," I said, hoping to scare her. If she thought I didn't want to eat lunch with her anymore, maybe she'd forget about those older kids.

She looked at me. Not with pity or with anger or even surprise. It was an expression I had never seen before. A new bland maturity. "Maybe this is best," Dilys said. "At least I'm not bored silly at lunch anymore. You should do that, too, Maxie."

"Do what?"

"Make new friends."

Dilys was anything but scared by my hollow threat. She was quitting being best friends! Suddenly I was furious, as furious as Todd had been with me earlier. If anybody should quit, it ought to be me! I had the *right* to quit our friendship! As always, Dilys beat me to the punch.

She left, closing the door behind her. I heard her speak to my mother, in the polite voice she used with grown-ups. No one would ever suspect that she had just dumped her best friend.

6

The next morning there was an assembly at Willow Springs. Instead of going on to Centreville High, all students got off at the elementary school. The buses would stay until the assembly was over to take the sixth-graders to the high school later.

Since the sixth-graders didn't have a classroom to go to first, we went directly into the gym. Ms. Terry and the other teachers prowled the floor in front of the bleachers, trying to take attendance.

I wanted to sit as far away from Dilys as I could. I waited until she found a seat next to Alison Mosconi. Then I went over to the other end of the bleachers. Where Katherine and Michelle were.

"Hi. Can I join you guys?" I asked.

Katherine looked up from the eye shadow compact she was showing Michelle. "Hi, Maxie. Where's Dilys? Is she sick today?"

"She's here someplace," I said vaguely.

70

"You're usually with her. Did you guys have a fight or what?"

"I just feel like sitting with somebody else for a change." I smiled, so they wouldn't guess Dilys had dumped me as her best friend. I didn't want people feeling sorry for me.

Katherine shifted over slightly. I managed to wiggle in. They had a bunch of makeup spread out on the bleacher seat between them.

"What's the program today? Does anybody know?" I chirped. You have to be cheerful when you're trying to make new friends.

"Some lady TV announcer," Michelle replied absently. "Hey, Kath, do you think this would look good on me?"

"Put some on." Katherine held her notebook up in front of Michelle's face like a shield. "The teachers aren't looking. Hurry up."

"What channel?" I said, sensing they forgot I was there.

Katherine stared at me. "What?"

"I said, what channel? The TV announcer. What channel is she from?"

"I don't know," Katherine said, somewhat irritated. "Seven, I think. Let's see, Michelle." She lowered the notebook. Michelle's eyelids were purple and sparkly. She looked like a circus performer. "Oooh, that looks great!" Katherine exclaimed.

"Yeah," I agreed. "It looks neat. Can I use some, too?" I didn't want to wear eye shadow, least of all glittery purple eye shadow, but that's what Katherine and Michelle were into these days, clothes and makeup. If I wanted to be friends with them, I'd have to do what they liked to do.

Katherine snapped the case shut with a final click. "I really don't want to waste it, Maxie. I just let Michelle try a little, but I want to save the rest to wear to the dance." She scooped the compact and other cosmetics into her purse.

"Oh, yeah. That stuff's hard to get," I said understandingly, but my glimpse into Katherine's purse revealed enough makeup to stock a department store. She certainly had plenty to spare. Then I said, "What dance? I haven't heard about any sixth-grade dance."

"Homecoming," Michelle answered.

"Sixth-grade homecoming? What's that?"

Katherine gave me her don't-you-know-anything expression. "Not sixth-grade homecoming. Centreville High homecoming. It's the first big dance of the year. Every high school has a homecoming weekend."

"Oh, a high school dance. The sixth-graders won't be allowed to go, will they?" I asked doubtfully. Bursting Katherine's dream bubble wasn't exactly the way to begin a new friendship.

Katherine flipped her hair back. "Why not? They let us enter the door-decorating contest. Why shouldn't we be allowed to go to the dance?"

The other classes started filing into the gym. Mr. Rice, the principal, introduced the guest speaker. The pretty news announcer was from channel seven. I nudged Katherine to tell her that she was right after all, but she and Michelle were playing hangman. I glanced over Katherine's shoulder to see the word Michelle had just figured out. *N-E-R-D*.

They meant me, I just knew it.

I never heard a word of the program, even though I always thought television work might be interesting. I was the nerd, believing I could be friends with girls like Katherine and Michelle. They'd been best friends as long as Dilys and I had been friends, maybe even longer. They needed me around like a car needed a fifth wheel.

That was one major problem with sixth grade. Most of the kids had known each other for years and they'd already paired off. All the good best friends were taken. My only hope was to wait for somebody to have a big blow-up with their best friend. Or I could go crawling back to Dilys.

I craned my neck to see her at the other end of the bleachers. She had her hand over her mouth, muffling a giggle. Alison must have said something funny. Dilys never looked over at me. Not once.

Forget Dilys. I was on my own.

It's hard sitting next to your enemy. I never realized that fact until we were back in room 228. My desk was next to Dilys'. Dilys didn't speak to me, and I didn't speak to her. During math and social studies, I kept sneaking glances at her to see if she was sneaking looks back at me, but she never was.

I accidentally dropped my pencil. It rolled under Dilys' desk.

"Ex-cuse me," I said with exaggerated politeness. "My pencil is under your desk. Could you reach it for me, please?"

With her shoe, Dilys scuffed the pencil to my side of the aisle, then went back to her class assignment.

I bent down to retrieve my pencil. "Hope you didn't hurt yourself," I muttered.

Lunchtime was a repeat of the morning. Once again, I found myself without anyone to sit with. Dilys waited until Ms. Terry had her back turned and then scooted over to the ninth-grade table where her new friends were waiting. Katherine and Michelle claimed one end of our table. Benjamin and Michael and the rest of the boys anchored the other end, leaving me to find a seat in the Pits, the uncool seats in between.

I wound up sitting next to Horst who read a science book while he ate his sandwich. I wished I had brought something to read. Nothing was more boring than eating without talking to somebody or watching TV. I found myself counting how many times I chewed each bite. Finally I decided to make conversation with Horst.

"Good book?" I asked.

He surfaced reluctantly. "Um."

"What's it about?" I pressed. I didn't really care if he was reading the phone book. I just wanted somebody to *talk* to.

Horst, I discovered, was not the type to make lunchtime small talk. When he spoke, it was in complete, grammatically perfect sentences and usually about something dull.

"Were you aware that a squirrel's nest is called a drey?" he said.

"No, I wasn't." I could have gone all day without hearing that little tidbit, but I was grateful that someone, even Horst, was talking to me.

"The males build nests, too," he added. "Those are known as buck dreys. Most people believe that squirrels nest in hollow trees, but it isn't true."

"I'm glad you set me straight, Horst. All my life I thought squirrels lived in hollow trees." I was beginning to feel a bit squirrelly myself.

A commotion at the other end of the table interrupted our fascinating conversation.

"What's going on?" I stood up so I could see better.

Benjamin tossed a lunch bag high into the air. I knew instantly it wasn't his. Michael caught the bag and pitched it back. I could see Ellen Dietzler standing by helplessly. It was her lunch. Benjamin and Michael were playing keep away with Ellen's lunch. Higher and higher the lunch bag went, until the flying sack finally caught Ms. Terry's attention.

She was up in a flash. "Who's lunch is that?" she demanded. "Benjamin? Is that Ellen's lunch? Stop fooling around or you'll sit in this chair next to me the rest of the week."

Benjamin thrust Ellen's lunch at her. "Here, take your slimy old lunch."

Ellen, who was the last straggler through the milk-only line, was looking for a place to eat. She'd made the mistake of checking out the boy's end of the table. Benjamin pounced, like a waiting panther. With her battered lunch, Ellen headed down the table to the empty "troublemaker" chair among the teachers. The other kids chanted, "Cooties, cooties!" and made barfing sounds.

Automatically I leaned forward as she passed behind me. And immediately wondered why I did it.

"It's very unlikely that Ellen Dietzler is infested

with head lice," Horst remarked to me. "We were all examined at the beginning of the year. If she had lice, she would have been sent to the nurse."

"What *are* you babbling about?"

"Cooties. That's a quaint expression for head lice, parasites that feed on warm-blooded animals by sucking blood and other juices — "

"Okay, okay. Please, no science lesson on parasites. My stomach can't take it." I wrapped up my uneaten sandwich. I wasn't hungry anymore, but I wasn't sure my sudden loss of appetite was entirely Horst's fault. A stray thought told me I ought to blame *myself*, but I dismissed that ridiculous idea.

What had I done? If anything, I was an innocent bystander being dumped on by the entire world.

Because it was raining, we had indoor recess. Ms. Terry organized a wild volleyball game, our class against Ms. Johnson's. With so many kids on each team, it was more like a free-for-all than a volleyball game. Instead of rotating in three even lines, we formed a solid square of players that went smack up against the net. Five or six kids would aim for the ball whenever it came sailing over to our side. Dilys and I stayed far apart, at opposite ends of the court. It was such a crazy game, nobody noticed that we weren't speaking to each other.

Gradually the players rotated until it was my

turn at the front of the net. I found myself next to Ellen. Her white-blonde hair clung in damp curls to her neck. It was a fun game, loud and boisterous, and our side was ahead.

The other team served the ball in our direction. It was hard to tell whether the ball would clear the net.

"Spike it! Spike it!" Benjamin Potter bellowed behind me.

Ellen and I both leaped for the ball at the same time, but somebody shoved us against the net and we missed the shot. The other side gleefully called out the score. They were winning now.

"Slimeball Dietzler missed!" Benjamin cried, outraged. "If it landed on your nose, you would have missed! Stupid girl!"

Beside me, Ellen concentrated intensely on the game. Benjamin's taunts went on and on. Finally I turned around and said to him, "I missed it, too. Why don't you tell me how stupid I am?"

"It was *her* shot!"

"It was aimed at both of us," I corrected. "Benjamin, just shut up."

Miraculously, he did. Ellen flicked me a grateful glance. Benjamin kept his big mouth buttoned until it was Ellen's turn to serve and then he let loose a string of smart remarks. He made Ellen so nervous, she couldn't even hit the ball out of our court. I thought she was going to cry, but she didn't. Ms. Terry ordered Benjamin to sit out the rest of the game, but it was too late. Benjamin spoiled what should have been a fun, silly game.

I wondered why I ever thought Benjamin Potter was cute. Ever since he started school at Centreville High, he had been obnoxious, always picking on somebody, usually Ellen. I guess Dilys wasn't the only one who had changed this year. Everyone but me had changed. I was still plain old boring Maxie Granville, the mole of Centreville High. A mole without friends, I might add.

To calm us down after that wild game, Ms. Terry read to us back in class. We had finished *Johnny Tremain*, and now we were reading a book about a girl lost in Alaska. Some wolves helped her. As I listened, I wished I were as brave as Julie, the girl in the story. If I were lost on the tundra, I'd probably starve to death. I'd be afraid of the wolves.

The book was so exciting, we asked Ms. Terry to read until it was time to go home. Soon we heard the other classes coming down the hall. Ms. Terry closed the book with a startled glance at the clock.

"I can't believe it's that late," she said. "Hurry, class. I don't want anybody missing their bus."

The buses were mostly filled by the time our class reached the loading zone in front of the school. We ran around like people in one of those old disaster movies, trying to find the right bus.

Amid the screaming and yelling, a wail made me spin around. Benjamin Potter had grabbed Ellen's knapsack and was pitching it to Michael.

"*This* is how you spike the ball," he said, tossing the knapsack just out of Ellen's reach.

Normally Ellen waited until Benjamin tired of picking on her, but now she was frantic. It was no joke to miss your bus. The drivers never knew if a kid went home in the middle of the day, so they didn't bother taking a head count. And there weren't any late buses for the sixth-graders at Centreville High.

Suddenly something in me snapped. I was sick of watching Benjamin torment Ellen. She hadn't done a thing to him, yet he ragged her from the minute she set foot in class until it was time to go home. Even worse, everyone in room 228 had joined his ugly cause. It was time somebody stood up for Ellen.

I marched over to Benjamin and snatched the knapsack in midarc. I gave it back to Ellen, who fled for her bus, which was first in the line with the engine already running.

"Why don't you pick on somebody your own I.Q.?" I said, disgusted.

Benjamin's eyes narrowed. "Look who's talking. Are you taking up for Slimeball Dietzler now, Granville? You're just as slimy as she is, then."

80

Racing for his own bus, he shouted, "Red alert! Red alert! Stay away from Maxie Granville!"

As I climbed the steps of my own bus, realization set in. Hard. Because I defended Ellen Dietzler, I was fair game for Benjamin and the rest of his goon squad. Now they'd add me to their victim list. Nobody would want to be friends with me. I was marked.

But then, I thought, finding an empty seat far away from Dilys Freeman, what did it matter? If all my so-called friends were changing into people I didn't like anymore, what was I losing?

7

"Life is unfair!"
— *Maxie Granville's Theory of Life*, Vol. II

The pizza was hot and gooey. I took a bite, then held the slice out. A string of cheese made a loopy bridge from my mouth to the pizza.

Todd took two slices, folded them over and began eating, a slice in each hand. He could make pizza disappear faster than anybody I knew. Dad said Todd was a two-fisted eater.

"Don't let me forget to save some for your mother," Dad said, reaching for a third slice. His vows to "lose a few" must have flown out the window.

"I'll put some on a plate for her." I cut a couple of big wedges, then stowed the plate in the microwave.

Mom was working tonight. The shop stayed open later on Thursdays anyway, but this evening a famous illustrator was appearing at The Rabbit Hole to autograph books. Mom and Lola had sent invitations to a zillion people and were expecting a big turnout. Mom even ordered a cake from the bakery and was fixing punch. Instead of cooking dinner for us, Dad brought home a giant deluxe pizza.

"Things have certainly been quiet around here lately," Dad remarked, looking at Todd.

"What do you mean?" Todd replied, wiping tomato sauce off his chin with the back of his hand. I had set the table with paper napkins but my brother was impossible to civilize.

"I don't see the regulars anymore. Gary, Boris. The driveway seems empty without three or four skateboarders to swerve around. Where've they been?"

"Rat's in my English class. I don't see Thrasher that much."

Rat and Thrasher were Todd's friends. Their real names were Gary and Boris, but they gave themselves nicknames when they became board freaks. Todd's nickname was Speed. Dad was right — Todd's friends hadn't been around to clean out our refrigerator the last few weeks.

"Well?" Dad prompted when Todd didn't say anything more.

"Well, what?"

"You three were inseparable. I thought those

skateboards were permanently welded to the bottoms of your shoes," Dad said, refilling our glasses with Coke. The only time we had soft drinks with dinner was when we had pizza.

"They've traded their skateboards for track shoes," Todd said with something like disgust.

Dad lifted an eyebrow. "Gary and Boris went out for track, eh? I was on the track team myself, back in the olden days. J-V and Varsity. My trophy's around here someplace — "

"You were on the track team?" Todd asked incredulously. I found it hard to believe myself. Dad puffed if he had to walk up more than two flights of stairs. I couldn't picture him running and jumping hurdles.

"Yes, your old man was actually on the track team! Once upon a time I was young myself. Not only was I a star runner, but in the summer I mowed lawns and in the winter I shoveled sidewalks. None of this hanging around malls, whining that there's nothing to do."

Across the table, Todd rolled his eyes upward. Every so often, Dad got on a kick about how when he was a teenager, back in the Dark Ages, kids had more get-up-and-go. They didn't slouch around on skateboards, wired to Walkmans. But I've seen pictures of Dad when he was a teenager. He had hair down to his shoulders and bangs hanging in his eyes! I wondered how he could *see* to mow a lawn!

But Dad didn't launch on a trip down Memory Lane. Instead he said to Todd, "You're in good shape. Why don't you try out for track, too?"

Todd sputtered Coke in his surprise. "You think I could be on the track team?"

"Sure, why not? You've been skateboarding for years. You have excellent coordination. Didn't Gary and Boris ask you to try out with them?"

Todd stared very hard at his glass. "No. I guess they thought I wouldn't be interested. They act different now. Like skateboarding is for babies. I can't explain it."

Picking the anchovies off my pizza, I realized why Todd blew up at me the other day. He really *had* lost his friends. He wasn't kidding. We were both in the same friendless boat.

"It's understandable," Dad said, nodding. "You boys are in high school now. Things *are* different, interests change. But you really ought to give it a shot, Todd. Don't hang back. These will be the best years of your life.

"If these are the best years of my life, I might as well give up now." But Todd was teasing, I could tell. His eyes had brightened when Dad suggested he go out for track. "So you think I have excellent coordination, huh?"

"Except on the rare occasions you take out the garbage — you always manage to drop something that doesn't pick up easily, like coffee grounds." Then Dad turned to me, "Where's your other half these days, Maxie? I haven't seen Dilys in ages."

"She has other interests, too," I said evasively. "She hangs around a crowd of ninth-graders."

"Why would ninth-graders want to hang around a sixth-grader?" Dad asked.

I shrugged. "They talk about drama and poetry and stuff."

Todd spoke up. "They've sort of adopted Dilys. You know, like a mascot. That Gail person is in my French class. She's weird, just like Dilys."

"Dilys is not weird," I said, wondering why I bothered to defend my ex-best friend. "She's a nonconformist." But then I realized what Todd had said. Dilys was only a *mascot*. Would her face be red if I told her that! But it would hurt her feelings, and I couldn't deliberately hurt anyone's feelings, not even a friend who'd dumped me.

"It's not the same without the old regulars cleaning out our refrigerator," Dad said wryly.

"I have other friends now," I said, hoping to get him off the subject. Before Dad could ask me about my new nonexistent friends, I began clearing the table. "Mom'll be home soon. Let's get this mess cleaned up."

"You and Dilys were like each other's shadows,"

Dad pursued. "I never saw one without the other."

Actually I was Dilys' shadow. Dilys would never be anyone's shadow, least of all mine. She'd never promoted me from assistant Fall Fairy.

Pounding my fist on my locker did not make it open, I found. Only dynamite would . . . or Dilys. But since Dilys and I had parted company, she no longer performed the service of opening my locker for me.

The first week I managed by draping my sweater on the back of my chair and stuffing my lunch in my desk. But today I needed a library book that was in my locker. I pounded the stubborn door again.

"There's a trick to it," a voice said behind me. It was Ellen. "I had trouble with mine, too, until I figured out this trick. Do you have your combination?"

I showed her my sweaty combination slip.

"Turn the dial toward the stairs first, then toward our class, then back to the stairs," Ellen instructed. "It's like the order we use in school. Stairs, class, stairs. Get it?"

Without worrying about right and left, I whirled the dial to each number, using Ellen's trick. It worked!

"Thanks," I said gratefully.

She smiled. "One good turn deserves another."

I didn't catch the real meaning of her remark until later when we were in the ESC. Ms. Terry selected me and Ellen Dietzler to feed Garcia for the next month. "You're both good with animals," Ms. Terry told us. "Instead of switching monitors every week, I've decided to let you two feed the rabbit for a whole month."

I wondered if she had paired Ellen with me on purpose, knowing I wouldn't call Ellen names or tease her.

"I'm glad she picked us," Ellen said as we got Garcia's food from the cabinet.

"Me, too. I wish I could feed him every day." The other sixth-grade classes took turns taking care of the rabbit on their days in the ESC.

Ellen shredded lettuce leaves. "Thanks for helping me yesterday. When Benjamin grabbed my knapsack."

"Thanks for showing me your trick." Then I added, "Benjamin is such a jerk. He wasn't so bad last year. I don't know what happened to him over the summer. I think his brain melted in the heat."

"Still, it was nice of you. Standing up for me that way. I thought I'd miss my bus. My mom wasn't home that day, so it would have been a long walk home."

I shrugged, embarrassed at the way Ellen was going on about it. "I'd do it for anybody."

Ellen fixed me with her pale blue eyes. "But you did it for me." Her tone carried a strong, hidden message. She implied that I risked not having any friends — ever — by sticking up for the sixth-grade outcast.

I had gone out on a limb for Ellen the day before, but I wasn't sure I wanted to be linked with her.

I looked at Ellen, *really* looked at her. She was pretty in a rabbity sort of way. She made good grades — not a brain, but not the class dummy, either. She was fairly good in sports, except when Benjamin Potter was on her case. And she was nice, maybe a little too eager, but always pleasant to everyone, kids and teachers alike.

Yet no one — absolutely no one — liked Ellen Dietzler. I didn't understand why everyone was so mean to her.

"I'm having a party Saturday," Ellen said. "Would you come?" Her eyes were practically pleading. I couldn't have turned her down if I'd already had an invitation to the White House Saturday.

"Yes, I'll come," I heard myself saying, figuratively crawling to the very tip of the limb.

I was actually going to the outcast's *house*. If word got around, I'd be branded forever. Then it dawned on me that other people would be there, too. Ellen probably had friends from another school, which was why she never seemed too upset when the kids here picked on her. I'd get to meet Ellen's other friends. Maybe they'd become my friends, too.

That night while I was helping my mother with the dinner dishes, I mentioned Ellen's situation.

"There's this girl in my class that nobody likes. She seems nice, really. I don't know why everybody picks on her," I said.

"Sometimes people can be cruel," Mom said. "But I think they do things like that more out of fear."

"What are they afraid of? This girl wouldn't hurt a flea."

"They aren't afraid of the person they're tormenting. They're really afraid of not being accepted, even if it means doing things they wouldn't ordinarily do. Fear makes people cowardly. You have to decide for yourself what is right."

I leaned against the stove, more confused than ever. If I was going to Ellen's house hoping to meet new friends, why didn't I count *Ellen* as a friend? What was I afraid of? Maybe I was just as cowardly as the kids who picked on Ellen.

Ellen Dietzler lived in one of the new houses behind what was left of our woods. I'd never realized she lived so close to me, but that was probably because she took a different bus to school.

It was just starting to rain when I parked Todd's bike in the Dietzlers' driveway. My bike was behind a pile of snow tires in our garage. Dilys and I used to ride to the pool or to the mall, but since school started I'd stopped riding mine. Todd's bike was available, so I borrowed his without telling him.

Like all the houses in the new development, the Dietzlers' house had a curious unlived-in look. There was a car in the driveway and a pot of bronze chrysanthemums on the porch, so I knew a family really lived there. But the lawn seemed raw and unfinished, and the scrawny, newly planted trees were braced with wires and sticks so they wouldn't fall over.

I went up to the front door and lifted the shiny brass knocker. Before I could let the knocker drop, the door opened.

Wearing new jeans and an expensive sweater, Ellen beamed at me. "Hi! Come in! I want you to meet my mom."

We walked through a foyer with thick beige carpeting and into a gleaming kitchen. A woman with hair only a little darker than Ellen's was putting parsley sprigs on a plate of crustless sandwiches.

"Mom, this is Maxie Granville," Ellen said. Her normally pale eyes were as bright as the chrome appliances. "Maxie, this is my mom."

"I love your house, Mrs. Dietzler," I said. "Everything's so new and shiny."

"The luster will wear off soon enough," she said with a laugh. "And call me Frances, will you?"

I didn't feel comfortable calling grown-ups by their first names. Dilys called her own *mother* by her first name sometimes, but then she was a nonconformist.

"We'll be downstairs," Ellen told her mother. "Come on, Maxie. The party's in the basement."

She led the way down a flight of steps. I expected to enter a rec room something like Dilys' — tiled floor and dark paneling. The Freemans kept a junky old television set down there.

But the Dietzlers' rec room was white with cream carpeting. An enormous television set was built into one wall. Shelves held stereo components and VCR tapes. Between the matched beige sofas was a glass-topped coffee table. On the other side of the room, a table and four chairs sat on a blue rug. Behind the table I glimpsed a tiny kitchen. The Dietzlers' rec room looked fancier than our living room at home.

Ellen slipped some music into the compact disc

player. I recognized the old Beatles tune. "This is my parent's CD," Ellen said, "but I like it. Sit down, Maxie. Mom will bring the food down in a minute."

I sat gingerly on the sofa facing the television wall. "This is really neat. You probably have kids over all the time, wanting to watch movies on that huge screen."

Ellen didn't reply. She batted at a bunch of helium balloons that had been tied to the back of one of the chairs. I noticed twisted crepe paper dangling from the light fixture, and gulped. The room was decorated for a *real* party. Was it Ellen's birthday? If it was, I hadn't brought her a present or a card or anything.

Always the realist, I decided to ask. "Ellen, you didn't tell me what kind of a party this is. I mean, is it your birthday?"

She straightened a pile of magazines on the coffee table. "No, it's not my birthday. Just a party." She smiled. "A Saturday afternoon get-together."

I settled back on the sofa. "I guess I'm early. The others aren't here yet."

"No, you're right on time. Finally, the food!" Ellen sprang up to help her mother, who was balancing a huge tray as she came carefully down the steps.

I got up and helped them unload the tray. Be-

93

sides the platter of sandwiches, Mrs. Dietzler had made nachos, fresh vegetables and dip, and two different kinds of brownies. Ellen placed dishes of peanuts and M&M's on the coffee table. From the tiny refrigerator under the counter, Mrs. Dietzler brought out about twenty soft drinks.

"Oh, I forgot the potato chips," Mrs. Dietzler said. "Ellen, run upstairs and get them."

Ellen pelted up the stairs as if she didn't want to miss a second of her party.

"The food looks great," I said to Ellen's mother, reaching for a nacho. There was enough for a small army. I hoped Ellen's other friends would arrive soon.

Mrs. Dietzler fussed with the napkin arrangement. She was a lot like Ellen, both kind of nervous. "I'm so glad you came today, Maxie. Ellen hasn't stopped talking about you and this party all week. You're the first friend she's brought home from school this year. I'm delighted that Ellen has finally found time to make friends."

I stopped, my hand halfway to the nacho plate. Ellen's mother didn't realize her daughter was the school outcast. She thought Ellen was too busy to make friends! She had no idea that everybody at school hated Ellen.

Just then Ellen clattered back down the steps. She carried a bag of potato chips and a videocassette of the latest Tom Cruise movie.

"Have you seen this yet?" she asked me.

"No. I've been dying to see it."

"Good. I'll put it in." Ellen switched off the compact disc player and slid the videocassette into the VCR.

"Shouldn't we wait for the others?" I asked uncertainly. "By the way, who else is coming?"

With the remote control, Ellen adjusted the volume. "There aren't any other guests," she said matter-of-factly. "I only invited you."

"Me? Just me?"

The truth hit me squarely in the pit of my stomach. Ellen didn't have any friends at another school. She didn't have any friends, anywhere, period. She and her mother went to all this trouble for one person. Me. I was the *only* guest at Ellen's party!

I wanted to cry. It was the saddest thing I had ever seen. No wonder Ellen was so excited. A friend finally came to her house.

"You sit over here," Ellen said. "You don't want to miss a single second of Tom Cruise."

I sat down, feeling like royalty. Ellen fixed us both Cokes. She clinked our glasses together, as if we were celebrating some grand occasion. I sipped my Coke with a lump in my throat.

When I got home, I went straight to my room and got out my *Theory of Life* notebook.

95

Life is unfair! I scribbled angrily over one entire page. The nicest girl in school was being treated like scum for no reason at all. The more I tried to figure out life, the less I understood how it worked!

Worst of all, I couldn't figure out where *I* fit in.

8

The note landed on my desk with a plop. Katherine dropped it on her way to the pencil sharpener. It was folded intricately, like a Chinese puzzle. I opened it carefully, trying not to rip the single page crowded with Katherine's round script. Katherine had never written me a note before. I wondered what she wanted.

Before reading it, I studied the pattern, so I could fold my own notes this way, too. Then I remembered I didn't have anybody to send notes *to* anymore. My ex-best friend still sat next to me, but she might as well be on Mars.

Dear Michelle, Katherine's note read. *Do you like Ms. Terry's necklace? I'm going to get one just like it. I heard some big kids say there isn't going to be a homecoming dance. They were really mad. I don't blame them! Did you hear about Maxie? She went to Slimeball Dietzler's house this weekend! I know because the boy who lives next*

*door to Dietzler is friends with Maxie's brother
and my brother. This boy wanted to know why
Todd Granville's bike was in front of some sixth-
grader's house. And Todd told this guy and my
brother that it wasn't him, it was his little sister.
Don't get near Maxie. You'll get slimed! Pass it
on —*

A hand shot out and snatched the note.

"That's mine," Michelle said. She wiped her fingers back and forth on her sweater, as if she'd
just touched something icky. "It has my name on
it, see? Katherine dropped it on your desk by
accident."

"Accidentally on purpose," I muttered. Katherine's aim was deadly. She could pitch a softball
better than any of the boys. She *wanted* me to
read that note. But why? To hurt my feelings? To
warn me that the campaign Benjamin Potter had
started against Ellen Dietzler would now include
me?

Darn Todd's big mouth. Why didn't he tell that
stupid kid, whoever he was, that it wasn't *his* bike
parked at the Dietzlers' Saturday afternoon, it
just *looked* like his bike. But no, he had to blab
to this kid and Katherine's brother that his little
sister borrowed his bike without permission. He
probably told them he was going to get back at
me, too. Brothers can't resist bragging to their
friends.

Someone stopped by my desk. I looked up, hoping for some irrational reason that it was Dilys flopping over in one of her outrageous outfits to apologize. Dilys would set Katherine and Michelle straight. Benjamin, too. Nobody would pick on me as long as I was Dilys Freeman's best friend.

But it wasn't Dilys. It was Ellen.

"Hi," she said, smiling widely. "I made you something." She drew a multicolored braided string from the pocket of her denim skirt. "It's a friendship bracelet."

Friendship bracelets were the rage in sixth grade. Ellen had woven the bracelet from silky embroidery floss in shades of purple, pink, and fuchsia. My favorite color combination. How did she know?

Ellen's smile faded. "You don't like the colors. I thought you did, because you wear that purple sweatshirt so much. I can make another one, in colors you like better."

A realistic person would think twice before accepting Ellen's gift. Being friends with Ellen Dietzler was like climbing the ladder of the water slide at our pool. There was always a line going up the ladder of the slide. Once you got to the top, there was no turning back. You had to go down the slide.

If I accepted Ellen's gesture of friendship I would have to accept the consequences. Nobody would like me. I would be an outcast by association. Slimeball Granville.

"No. It's perfect," I said. "I love it." The bracelet felt weightless in my palm. If I put it on, it would carry more weight than an iron chain. I held my wrist out. "Will you put it on me?"

That was the thing about friendship bracelets. You couldn't put them on by yourself. Someone else had to tie the knot.

Ellen flushed with pleasure as she secured the bracelet around my right wrist. "Is it too tight?" she asked.

"No. It's fine." For an instant, I considered hiding the bracelet under the cuff of my sweater. But it wouldn't do any good. Everyone around me — including Dilys — watched, goggle-eyed, as Ellen tied the bracelet around my wrist.

It was official. I was Ellen Dietzler's friend.

My life as an outcast with Ellen wasn't much different than my ordinary life without friends. Only now when nobody asked me to sit with them at lunch, I knew it was because I was with Ellen. But at least *she* wanted to sit with me at lunch.

She waited for me outside the classroom in the mornings, so we could walk into room 228 together. She saved me a seat at lunch, in the ESC, and in the gym back at Willow Springs Elementary when we had another assembly. I was surprised she didn't transfer to my bus route so we could sit together on the bus to and from school.

Benjamin Potter dubbed us the Slimeball Twins. "Don't get near them," he cautioned everyone within a fifty-mile radius. "Or you'll get double-slimed." The kids in class gave Ellen and me a wide berth wherever we went. It was like being on a separate planet. I wondered how Ellen had stood the isolation as long as she had.

Of course my friendship with Ellen didn't escape Dilys' notice. She stopped me one rainy lunch period outside the cafeteria. Gail, her ninth-grade friend, thrust a clipboard under my nose.

"Sign this," Gail urged.

"She can't sign it," Dilys informed her. "She's only a sixth-grader."

"Same as you, Dilys Freeman," I retorted. "In case you forgot. What is it, anyway?"

The older girl answered. "It's a petition for a fall dance. We can't have a homecoming because we didn't have a senior class last year, so there weren't any old grads coming back for homecoming weekend. This is the first year we have a senior class. But that's no reason not to let us have a dance. If we get enough signatures, they'll have to give in."

"So why can't I sign?" I said. "A name's a name."

Dilys grinned. "Yeah, why not? You sign and then I'll sign."

I scribbled my signature on the paper. I didn't really care about a fall dance. Things like that were important to Katherine and Michelle, not to me. But I wanted to show Dilys that I didn't always take the safe, sure road.

Maybe she knew that already because she said confidentially, "I hope you know what you're doing, Maxie."

"I just signed the petition, that's all." My heart flip-flopped. Did Dilys want to be friends again?

"I mean with Ellen Dietzler."

"What about Ellen?"

"You know what I mean." She cast a sideways glance at Gail, who was busy buttonholing more signers. I guess Dilys didn't want her ninth-grade friend to think she was involved with lowly sixth-grade problems.

"What do you care what I do?" I flung back over my shoulder. The bell rang and I had the rare satisfaction of walking away from Dilys before she could say anything. For once I had the last word.

The satisfaction didn't last, though. Upstairs in room 228 my entrance was greeted by now-familiar stony glances and one lone smile. Ellen's. *Did* I know what I was doing, being Ellen Dietzler's only friend? Was it worth the risk?

* * *

It rained all week. By Friday Willow Springs, normally a little creek, overflowed its banks and rushed into the streets. Our front yard became a swamp. Todd, who had track practice despite the weather, came home smelling like wet sweat socks. His shoes never dried and stank to high heaven.

Disaster struck Saturday morning. Mom left early to open the shop. Dad and Todd and I were sitting around, eating a late breakfast, when the phone rang. Dad answered it. I could hear Mom's hysterical voice shrieking at the other end.

"We'll be right over," Dad said and hung up. To us he announced, "Your mother's store flooded. Grab buckets, paper towels, rags, mops . . . everything you can to soak up water."

Five minutes later, I sat among a jumble of mop handles, buckets, and Dad's Wet-Dri shop vacuum in the backseat of the car. In my lap I held a basket with instant coffee, the sweet rolls left over from breakfast, and a Thermos of juice. Cleaning up a flood sounded like backbreaking work. I figured we'd need all the energy we could get.

The Rabbit Hole was located in a new shopping center about fifteen minutes from our house. Besides Mom and Lola's bookstore, there was a record shop, a store that sold nothing but quilts and pillows, a gift shop, and an Italian sub shop. The rest of the stores were still vacant.

Dad parked the car, and we splashed through standing water. The rain had stopped, but gray clouds with tattered edges barely cleared the rooftops.

When Dad opened the door of the shop, I expected water to come gushing out. Mom stood in the middle of the soggy carpet, trying to move a heavy bookcase. Her face was streaked with tears. Lola, Mom's friend and partner, was on her knees, throwing wet books into a box.

"Relief workers," Lola said when she caught sight of us.

"Everything is ruined!" Mom wailed to Dad. "We've lost everything!"

He went to her and put his arm around her. Todd and I looked at each other. Did this mean we were broke? I knew Dad and Mom had sunk all their savings, minus Todd's and my college funds, into starting this bookstore.

"Now, now," Dad soothed. "It's not as bad as it looks."

Mom pulled away. "What do you mean it's not as bad as it looks? Water is everywhere! The books are ruined! People don't buy wet books!"

Dad surveyed the damaged ceiling. Water had soaked through, leaving a brownish stain. "I'll call the owner of the building so he can inform his insurance company right away. Then I'll see if I can put a temporary flashing over the leak." He patted Mom's cheek. "Don't fret, hon. These things happen. New building . . . all this rain . . . when the roof is fixed, it'll be able to withstand a hurricane."

But my mother seemed rooted to the spot, wiping water off the top of a bookcase that just got wet all over again because the ceiling was still dripping. Dad left to find a ladder, after instructing me and Todd to start cleaning up. Todd, who thought he was next in command in Dad's absence, put me on the mop-and-bucket detail.

"What are you going to do?" I asked him.

"Move furniture." With his shoulder to the bookcase, he shoved, but it wouldn't slide over wet carpet.

"Wait a minute!" I said. "This is not going to work."

Todd quit shoving. "You have a better idea, Einstein?"

"We need a system." I considered the situation.

Actually the damage was not as widespread as Mom made it sound. Only the bookcases at the front of the store were drenched. These held picture books, which were the more expensive books in the store, but there weren't as many of them on the shelves because of their odd sizes. And most of these were protected by the overhang of the shelves. The carpet was the worst. Our shoes made squelching noises underfoot.

"The carpet will have to be ripped up first," I said. "Which means moving all the bookcases to the back of the store. That's your job, Muscles."

"Thanks a lot," Todd said. "These bookcases only weigh about a thousand pounds."

"I'll help," Lola offered.

"Mom, you and I will start moving the books to the back room."

"Why bother?" Mom said drearily. "We might as well just throw them out."

"Not all of them. Most of them are just damp. They'll probably dry a little crinkly." Suddenly I had an idea. "You know what you can do? Put them out front in a big basket as freebies. People love free stuff, even if it's not in perfect shape. Freebies attract customers, too."

Mom brightened a little. "That's a terrific idea, Maxie!"

With a plan, the cleanup operation went much smoother. It was still hard work, hauling books, moving ten-ton bookcases, and then ripping up wet carpet, but Lola put on the radio and I set up the refreshments on the cashier's counter. By the time Dad got back with the ladder, we looked less like victims of a tornado and more like people with a purpose.

The hole on the roof wasn't as big as Dad had thought it was. He could patch it temporarily until the carpenter got there. He left again for the hardware store. This time when he returned, he also brought his camera and lunch. The owner of the Italian deli, whose store had escaped damage, generously donated subs, potato chips, and drinks.

We sat in the stockroom, the only dry part of the shop, and ate.

"Maxie had a wonderful suggestion," Mom said to Dad. "Put the not-so-bad books out front as giveaways."

"She organized the mopping-up, too," Lola added.

Todd patted me on the back. "I always knew you were good for something, Moondoggie."

"I hate that name." I threw a potato chip at him.

"How about Munchkin?"

"I hate that even more. Besides, you promised not to call me that, ever," I reminded him. "I hear enough of it at school."

Todd defended his fellow high-school students. "They just say it to be funny."

"It isn't, though." Names hurt, I had learned.

"Maxie isn't the type to have a nickname," Mom said musingly. "The name she has suits her — no-nonsense. The sensible one in the family. What would we do without her?" She reached over and hugged me. I felt better than I had in a long time. It was nice to be appreciated. Maybe being realistic wasn't so bad, after all!

Dad picked up his camera. "I have to take pictures for the insurance company."

"Hey, you know what?" I said, inspired. "Let's take a family portrait. Isn't this a special occasion?"

Mom grinned at Dad. "Why not? How many flooded bookstores will we clean up in our lifetimes?"

We posed out front. Lola snapped the picture. I bet my face was goofier than Todd's. For the first time in ages, I felt I belonged in my family.

Mom and I went back to sorting books.

"Maxie, how come I never see Dilys anymore? Did you two have a fight?" Mom asked.

"Not exactly." I didn't want to admit that Dilys dumped me because I was dull and boring.

"That girl hasn't been the same since her parents split up," Mom said.

"What do you mean?" Dilys never acted like the divorce bothered her. She claimed she saw more of her father than she did before the divorce.

"It's a big adjustment. Especially at Dilys' age. She's very impressionable."

"Nothing makes an impression on Dilys," I maintained. "She's a nonconformist, remember? She makes her own impressions."

"You and Dilys have been friends a long time. But maybe it's good you're getting some breathing room. Dilys is a strong influence."

I hefted a stack of books. Mom noticed my purple bracelet.

"That's pretty," she commented. "Where did you get it?"

"Oh, this girl gave it to me." I wore Ellen's bracelet but I still couldn't admit that I was friends with the school outcast. I changed the subject hastily.

"This store's never going to make us rich, is it?" I asked my mother.

She dried the dust jacket of a book with a rag. "Probably not. Why?"

"I thought that was the whole idea of opening this shop. You told Dad we'd be on Easy Street and he could retire."

"I was just kidding, Maxie. You don't really believe we'll become millionaires selling picture books, do you?"

"Now I don't. But I thought that was why you quit your job and started this shop."

My mother spread the pages of a Dr. Seuss book and put it on the radiator to dry. "I'll tell you why I did it. Because I knew it would make me happy. Opening a bookstore started out as a joke between me and Lola. Soon we realized we had to try it. I doubt we'll ever be rich. We'll be thrilled if we break even. But we'll be rich in experience, in the long run." I knew she spoke the absolute truth. Sure the shop had given her its share of headaches — today's disaster probably the biggest headache of all — but Mom *did* seem happier now than when she was a secretary.

"Suppose you don't break even," I said. "Suppose we lose all our money."

"Suppose we do?" Mom said lightly. "At least we will have tried. Some risks are worth taking. That's what makes life exciting. Let's see if Todd and Lola are ready to rip carpet."

I followed her out to the front of the store with her words ringing in my ears. *Some risks are worth taking.*

Was it worth the risk being friends with Ellen Dietzler? Until I figured out the answer, I couldn't in all honesty wear Ellen's friendship bracelet . . . or face myself in the mirror.

9

"When life hands you a lemon, make lemonade."
— *Maxie Granville's Theory of Life*, Vol. II

Centerfest! Centreville High's Fall Fling! Dance to the live sounds of Wipeout! October 29 at 7:00. Tickets go on sale Friday in the cafeteria."

Dilys dabbed orange paint on the leaves fluttering around the announcement. So far she had made five posters during our free period.

I watched as Dilys traced leaf-veins with a fine-tipped black marker. The library book I was reading was okay but not thrilling enough to keep me glued to the pages. We weren't required to read during free period, although Ms. Terry preferred it. Some of the kids were cleaning out their desks or copying over homework assignments. A few drew pictures. Ms. Terry didn't care what we did, so long as we were quiet.

My attention kept wandering across the aisle to Dilys' desk, which was cluttered with poster board, markers, and poster paint.

We hadn't spoken to each other since the day I signed the dance petition. The high school kids finally got their wish — they were having a formal dance after the football game, in place of a homecoming dance. Wonder of wonders, Todd was actually on the entertainment committee. The live band had been his idea, instead of hiring a deejay. The dance was all the school talked about these days.

Now Dilys lettered her signature at the bottom of the completed poster. *Poster designed by Dilys Freeman, room 228.*

I leaned over, unable to resist a comment. "Trying to make a point?"

She glanced up at me sharply, as if she wasn't sure who had spoken. Maybe she had forgotten the sound of my voice.

"Actually, yes," she replied.

"What? Showing off your artwork?"

"Hardly. Everybody knows about the Willow Spring Annex and where it is. When they see 'room 228' they'll know a sixth-grader made the poster."

"Why don't you just put 'Dilys Freeman, sixth-grader'?"

Her expression would have withered one of

those huge California redwood trees. "Honestly, Maxie. Do you think I'm that juvenile? 'Room 228' gets the message across."

"What message?"

"The dance." Dilys jabbed her finger at the word "Centerfest!" "Sixth-graders aren't allowed to go. I want the rest of the school to feel guilty about leaving us out."

"You want to go to a high school dance?" I asked unbelievingly. Dilys might be a nonconformist, but she hadn't totally lost her mind. At least, I didn't *think* she had.

"Not particularly. But I hate the way they left us out."

"It's *their* dance," I said, feeling as if we'd had this argument before.

"It's a *school* dance," Dilys corrected. "Are we in this school or not?" Checking the clock, she said, "I guess I don't have time to start a new poster. I told Gail I'd make twenty. That's the trouble with such a big school — you have to make a zillion posters."

The mention of her ninth-grade friend rankled me. I was already in a rotten mood, for some reason. "How does it feel to be the poster assistant?"

"What are you talking about?" Naturally Dilys wouldn't remember the time years ago she had me convinced she was the Fall Fairy.

"I'm surprised your *friends* won't let you come to their dance, after you've done all this work for them."

Dilys chose to ignore my words, latching on to my sour tone instead. "It's not like you to be sarcastic, Maxie," she said. "You used to be so nice."

"Don't you mean dull? Maybe I'm changing," I said. "Maybe I'm finally getting out of my rut, like you told me."

"Okay, class," Ms. Terry said, collecting the papers she had finished grading. "Free period is over. Put away your activities. I'm going to pass back last week's math tests. I think we need to spend more time on sets and subsets. As a group, you didn't do that well on the test."

A general groan rose from the class. The two weeks we'd spent on sets and subsets had been a real grind.

"While I'm passing back your tests, I'm going to hand out a ditto of review problems." Ms. Terry picked up a sheaf of dittos. "Ellen," she said. "Would you hand these out?"

Ellen slowly left her desk and went to the front of the room. I knew she hated to do anything that called attention to herself. Life was more bearable for her now that she had a friend, but the kids still picked on her unmercifully. They picked on me, too, though not as much. Comments and insults sort of glanced off me, as a by-product of hanging around Ellen.

Ms. Terry began returning test papers at my end of the room first. I briefly noted the C I had received — I was more interested in what would happen when Ellen gave Benjamin Potter a ditto. He'd been awful to her lately.

True to form, he flicked the ditto off his desk. Ms. Terry didn't see — she was busy explaining to Horst why he didn't get an A-plus this time. Usually she was aware of disturbances in the room. Benjamin said she had eyes in the back of her head; she could talk to one kid and snap her fingers at another without ever turning around. But Horst was whining pretty loudly over his A-minus.

"Pick it up," Benjamin told Ellen. Ellen bent and picked up the paper. She put it on his desk. Again he flicked it off. "I thought I told you to pick it up."

"I did," Ellen said. "You threw it down."

"I didn't, either. You don't know how to hand out a simple piece of paper." Benjamin sat back, smirking. "Now pick it up."

I leaped up, disgusted with the whole business. "PICK IT UP YOURSELF, POTTER, YOU LAZY BUM!"

The entire class, including a stunned Ms. Terry,

swiveled to stare at me. Benjamin Potter's jaw dropped about four feet.

"Maxie!" Ms. Terry exclaimed in astonishment. "What on earth has gotten into you?"

"It's not me, it's Benjamin," I said, not caring a bit that I was being a big squealer. "He's giving Ellen a hard time."

Ms. Terry could be very stern when she wanted. "It is my job to maintain order in this classroom, Maxie, not yours. There was no call to scream as you just did. You will stay in during recess and write sentences." Then she turned to Benjamin. "I don't know what was going on but I'm sure you were instigating something. You will stay in also."

Benjamin shrugged. Writing sentences wasn't much of a punishment — more like part of his daily routine. Since he started sixth grade, Benjamin was forever staying after or staying in during recess to write a hundred sentences.

When recess time came, the class filed out. Dilys paused by my desk.

"You really *have* changed, haven't you?" Her voice held a tinge of admiration. I wondered if Dilys was interested in being friends again because I got in trouble. Then I was mad at myself for feeling hopeful at the thought. If Dilys was tired of the old, dull, realistic Maxie, she wasn't going to have a shot at the new version. *Was* there a new version?

Ms. Terry stayed in with me and Benjamin. I was very nervous. I had never been asked to stay in before.

"Benjamin, I want you to write one hundred times 'I will not act up in class.' Maxie, I want you to write 'I will not shout in class,' fifty times."

"Hey, no fair! How comes she gets to write fifty sentences and I have to write a hundred?"

"Because," Ms. Terry answered, "this is Maxie's first offense. And last, I hope." She smiled at me, and I felt better.

Benjamin fired dagger-looks across the room at me. When Ms. Terry wasn't looking, I stuck my tongue out at him. I wasn't afraid of him. Not anymore.

At lunchtime, Ellen gave me an entire pack of Twinkies in gratitude.

"You didn't have to do it. Get yourself in trouble and everything, over me."

"Somebody had to put that bully in his place," I said, accepting the Twinkies. "I can't eat both of these. We'll share, okay?"

"You're really something, Maxie," Ellen said. "I never had a friend like you before." I wasn't sure Ellen ever had a friend before *period*, but it was nice to hear her vote of confidence. Dilys never said things like that to me, not once in all the years we were best friends.

When I saw Todd enter the cafeteria with his friends, I remembered a message I was supposed to give him from Mom. It meant breaking our mutual agreement, but I figured he would make an exception for a direct order from Mom.

Letting Ms. Terry know where I was going, I left the sixth-grade table and went over to Todd's table. His eyebrows wiggled ominously, telling me to scram. When I didn't, he snapped, "You're in enemy territory, *Munchkin*."

He promised not to call me that! Angrily I said, loudly enough for everyone within five tables to hear, "*Mom* said to tell you to come straight home tonight. She has to work late, and she doesn't want me home by myself." I made it sound like I was too frail and delicate to be home alone a second without my big brother around.

"Awwwww," one of Todd's friends said. "Isn't that cute? Toddie-pooh has to baby-sit a Munch-kin."

Todd's face burned. I could feel the heat from where I was standing, which was safely out of swatting range. "I have an entertainment committee meeting after school," he said through clenched teeth.

"I can't help that," I sang cheerfully. "Mom said

for you to be home when I got home." I smiled, trying to seem even littler and more helpless.

"The dance committee is more important than watching some dumb Munchkin!" His face was splotchy. I couldn't tell which he was more upset about, having me show up at his table or having to go home directly after school. I did *not* like being called a "dumb Munchkin," even in front of a bunch of nerdy ninth-graders.

In for a penny, in for a pound, Dad sometimes said. Recklessly I added, "I don't know why you're killing yourself for the dance. You don't even have a date. I heard you on the phone last night — Mary Jane Erwin turned you down flat!"

Immediately Todd's friends began razzing him. I fled back to my own table before Todd could strangle me. My blood tingled in my veins. First Benjamin and now Todd! Both of them had it coming. I had never known it felt so good to stand up for myself, even against dangerous odds.

Little did I know my rashness would result in an uprising, the Big Kids versus the Munchkins.

Todd waited two days to get back at me.

At home he bided his time, pretending to be the same easy-going Todd Granville, even letting me borrow his bike to ride over to Ellen's house. Ellen's mother called my mother to invite me to dinner. I was glad for the invitation — I didn't think I could stand another evening of Todd's over-politeness at the supper table.

The surprise attack came on Thursday, right after lunch. The sixth-graders had a five-minute head start at the beginning of the lunch period so we wouldn't get squashed in the serving lines, but all the students left at the end of the lunch shift at the same time.

Because there was always a huge crush of kids leaving the cafeteria at once, moving against the crowd surging in, Ms. Terry and the other sixth-grade teachers waited until we were out in the atrium to line us up.

On this particular day, Todd came up to me as we were leaving the cafeteria.

"Come here, I want to show you something," he said.

"I can't. I have to go with my class."

"This'll only take a second." He grabbed my elbow and propelled me through the crowd. Around the corner we sailed, to the banks of yellow lockers.

"Is it in your locker?" I asked, wondering what he wanted to show me.

"Yes."

A few ninth-graders opened their lockers, retrieved or put away books, then slammed the doors shut to rush to their next class. Todd literally dragged me to one of the tall, free-standing lockers and began twirling the dial.

"Todd, I have to get back to class — "

He flung open the door. "Look in there, Maxie. And you'll see it."

"I don't see anything." I leaned into the interior of Todd's smelly locker. "Todd — "

Suddenly I felt his hands at my back. He shoved me into his locker and slammed the door! I was trapped in my brother's locker!

"Todd!" I screamed, pounding on the metal door. "Let me out of here! Todd!"

Silence. He had gone.

It wasn't totally dark in the locker. Vents at the top and bottom let in both air and light. But not enough of either, especially air. The fumes from Todd's gym shoes would suffocate a moose. Small as I was, I couldn't stand up straight. My head bumped the shelf above, so I had to keep my knees bent, which made my legs ache.

"Todd! Let me out of here!"

Laughter exploded outside the locker. People were laughing at the dumb Munchkin stuck in the locker.

"Todd!" I screamed.

"Coming through," I heard a man say. Keys jingled outside the locker, then there was the sound of a key being fitted into the lock set inside the combination dial.

121

The locker door opened. I stumbled out on cramped legs. A Centreville High vice-principal glared at me. The kids behind him giggled.

"One of our Annex students," he said with some surprise. "How did this happen, young lady?"

It was the perfect opportunity to get back at Todd, but good. Still, he was my brother and this man looked mad enough to flog whoever was responsible.

"I don't know," I said lamely. "I just . . . fell in. And the door shut behind me. It was an accident."

"An accident, eh?" The vice-principal didn't believe my weak excuse for a minute. Just then another man appeared on the scene and mumbled something about problems in the television studio. "All right," the vice-principal said to me. "You don't seem to be hurt. Go back to your class, young lady. Okay, people, the show's over. Wherever you're supposed to be this period, get moving."

I ran all the way upstairs to room 228. Ms. Terry had sent Ellen to the girls' room to find me. She accepted my explanation of being "unavoidably detained."

The problems with the Big Kids didn't stop there. The "attacks" of Munchkin Pats tripled. The next day, out by the flagpole, Benjamin Potter was knocked down — deliberately — by a bunch of tenth-grade boys. He hit the pavement hard enough to skin his knee right through his jeans.

"Creeps!" he yelled at the retreating boys, almost in tears. In class, Ms. Terry came to the rescue with wet paper towels, iodine, and a Band-Aid.

"I'd like to show them we're not Munchkins," Benjamin said, trying to be brave about the iodine.

"I'm sure they didn't mean to push you," Ms. Terry consoled. She hadn't seen the incident.

But a lot of us had. Those boys pushed Benjamin down on purpose.

In a way, I was glad to see Benjamin Potter getting a taste of his own medicine. Now he knew how it felt to be picked on. But he was right about one thing — the sixth-graders needed to show the Big Kids we were not Munchkins. There must be a way to use this incident to our advantage. My father always said when you're handed a lemon, make lemonade.

But how? I wondered. In stories, there was always a leader, a hero, to help the underdogs. That's what we needed. A sixth-grade hero.

I could be that hero, maybe. Some heros were very unlikely, like Johnny Tremain and Julie of the Wolves. I could show the Big Kids our class meant business and at the same time show the class I was no longer dull, average Maxie. As much as I wanted to be the hero, my realistic side cropped up and reminded me that I wasn't really the type.

I looked over at Ellen Dietzler. She was at the pencil sharpener. Michael was in line behind her, poking her with his own pencil.

There was our hero. I only had to convince Ellen she was hero material. And think of a plan.

10

"Not all heroes are brave."
— *Maxie Granville's Theory of Life,* Vol. II

The plan to get back at the Big Kids and make Ellen a hero at the same time came to me in the ESC.

It was the greatest idea I've ever had, a Dilys-Freeman-type idea, only *I* dreamed it up all by myself, without Dilys' help. It was such a *daring* plan, that the thought of pulling it off made me tremble. But we *could* do it.

Actually Ms. Terry deserved part of the credit. She was the one who announced that we would be learning more about animal behavior in science. Only instead of doing reports from books, we would have live specimens to observe.

Crickets and chameleons, to be exact. Lots of them. Hundreds of crickets and those little lizards that change colors.

When Ms. Terry told us we would be starting the science unit at the end of next week, when the animals were expected to arrive, the old light bulb went on over my head.

The only thing I had to do now was convince Ellen. While we were feeding the rabbit was as good a time as any.

As I poured dry pellets into Garcia's dish, I dithered over how to approach Ellen. She would never deliberately break the rules. Neither would I, for that matter. If we got caught it meant Big Trouble for both of us.

Then I remembered what Mom said about quitting her safe, sure job to gamble on the bookstore. When Mom talked about taking risks, I know she didn't mean doing something as crazy as my scheme. But Ellen and I both had been taking the safe, sure route for years and where had it gotten us? My best friend dumped me to hang around older kids, and Ellen became the target of the entire sixth grade. If this plan turned out the way I hoped it would, then it was definitely a risk worth taking.

Ellen came over with a dish of fresh water and a carrot for Garcia. Benjamin stuck his foot out in the aisle and tripped her. The water spilled all over the front of Ellen's sweater.

Ms. Terry saw the incident. "Benjamin, how many times do I have to tell you to keep your hands — and feet! — to yourself? Apologize to Ellen this instant."

"I'm sorry you're so wet," he mumbled insincerely, smirking at Michael.

"That's better," said Ms. Terry, though it really wasn't. Ellen's sweater was still soaked.

I spoke up. "I think Ellen should go to the girls' room to dry her sweater with some paper towels. I'll go with her and help. Okay, Ms. Terry?"

"Yes. Of course." Ms. Terry handed us the hall pass.

In the girls' room there were two sophomores smoking in the end stall. I yanked a wad of paper towels from the container on the wall, ignoring them.

"Aren't you tired of Benjamin Potter picking on you?" I said, dabbing at Ellen's sopping sweater. "And getting away with it?"

"Ms. Terry always yells at him," Ellen said. "She makes him stay after almost every day, writing sentences. It's not her fault Benjamin's such a brat."

"But he's turned everybody against you! You must hate him!"

"Nobody liked me before Benjamin started acting so mean to me," Ellen stated truthfully. Her words stabbed me with guilt. Maybe the kids didn't pick on her last year but nobody acted like her friend, either. Including me.

The sophomores flushed their cigarettes and left, but not before one of them remarked, "The little babies have to use the potty."

Her infuriating comment reminded me of my crusade.

"Wouldn't you like to get back at Benjamin?" I asked Ellen.

"Why? What good would it do? He'd just pick on me even more. At least this way I know what to expect."

Ellen was the exact opposite of Dilys Freeman. Dilys didn't take guff from anybody. Ellen didn't dare break a single rule, even if people like Benjamin walked all over her.

Maybe, I thought, watching her ruefully blot her sweater, Ellen didn't think much of herself. Dilys had a high opinion of herself as a person. She even admitted she was perfectly happy with herself, when she promised me she wouldn't change.

The ones who needed to change — Ellen and me — were afraid. Moles and rabbits weren't exactly hero material. But if we worked *together*, we could give each other moral support. It was time to stop following the safe road and strike a path of our own.

Putting my hand on her arm, I said, "Ellen, I have a plan that will let everybody in the sixth grade know how terrific you are." Despite Ellen's

128

unbelieving expression, I plowed ahead. "Not only that, but the big kids won't humiliate us anymore." Like the rest of us, Ellen had had her share of Munchkin Pats.

"You *are* joking, aren't you?"

I shook my head. "That's the beauty of this plan — we can kill two birds with one stone. It's foolproof, practically."

"It's the 'practically' that worries me." Ellen chewed her bottom lip. "Somebody *could* get in trouble, right?"

"Not if *you* do it. Success is almost one hundred percent guaranteed if you do it."

Ellen stopped blotting her sweater and blinked at me. "Do what? And why me? Why are you doing this, Maxie? I know the kids have started bothering you, too, but they'd stop if you found other friends."

That was the thing about Ellen. She really meant what she said, even if it caused her to lose her only friend.

"I don't want other friends," I said, with only a small twinge. It still hurt that Dilys didn't like me anymore, but not as much. "You're my friend. And because you're my friend I want to help you. I want to see Ellen Dietzler become the Sixth-Grade Hero."

Her eyes grew wide. "The — what?" she whispered.

"The Sixth-Grade Hero. You can do it, Ellen. It's a little risky, but some risks are worth taking. Do you want to hear my plan?"

She took a deep breath. Her eyes met mine and I saw the faintest spark of change.

"Yes," she said.

The next step involved spreading the plan to key people in our class. Katherine, Michelle, Michael . . . and Benjamin.

I considered letting Dilys in on the scheme. She'd be a good ally. Dilys was braver than anyone I knew. The next day on the bus to school, we sat next to each other. Not by choice but because there weren't any other seats.

Dilys was writing a note. Without sparing me a glance, she finished writing and then folded the note like one of those Japanese paper sculptures. I wondered if Katherine had taught Dilys how to fold paper that way. More likely, Dilys was the one who'd taught Katherine. The note was addressed to Gail, the red-haired ninth-grader Dilys ate lunch with. I decided then and there that Dilys could not be trusted with such an important secret. If she blabbed to her ninth-grade friends, it was all over. Secrecy was vital to the plan.

At school I found Michelle at her locker. For once Katherine was not hovering around.

"Hey, Michelle." I lowered my voice conspiratorially. "Guess what I heard on the bus?"

"What?" She didn't seem very interested, but she wasn't screaming "Slimeball!" either.

"A kid — a sixth-grader — has figured out a way to get back at the older kids in this school."

"Get back at them for what?"

"You know. Munchkin Pats. Being called babies all the time. Leaving us out of stuff, like the contest. And the dance."

"We got in the contest," she pointed out.

"But not the dance." I knew Michelle and Katherine were really disappointed to be shut out of their first high school dance. It was a sore point with them.

"Yeah." She sounded resentful. "So. Who is this mysterious person?"

"I can't tell you," I whispered. "The person's identity must be kept absolutely secret, or they might get expelled. The plan is dynamite. But the person needs help. Can we count on you?"

"Who *is* it?" Michelle persisted. "Come on, Maxie. You can tell me. Is it Dilys? It's Dilys, isn't it? I thought you two had a big fight."

I figured it wouldn't hurt to let her think Dilys and I were friends again. When I revealed the identity of the true Sixth-Grade Hero, Michelle and the others would be doubly dumbfounded. And that might work in Ellen's favor.

"Are you in or not?" I said, suddenly becoming businesslike. "We need kids who aren't afraid of taking risks."

"I'll do it if Katherine does."

That I expected. "Okay. We're going to have a meeting during recess tomorrow. Don't breathe a word of this to anyone. I'll contact the others. They've been specially chosen by our leader."

"Leader?" Michelle giggled. "A sixth-grade leader?"

"Don't you think it's time we had one?" Leaving Michelle with that thought, I rushed off to find Michael.

Michelle and Katherine were fairly easy to recruit. The boys would be tougher. Once Michael quit pretending to wipe slime off his arms, he listened to my pitch. The mystery of the Sixth-Grade Leader intrigued him. Katherine had liked the idea of being "handpicked" by the secret leader, and she joined without any hassle.

I saved the toughest recruit for last.

By the time I convinced Michelle, Michael, and Katherine, it was time to go inside room 228. Signing up the last volunteer would have to wait until recess. *If* Benjamin wouldn't have to stay in and write sentences. Miracle of miracles, he managed to stay out of trouble the whole morning.

Today was a free play day. We didn't have to form teams and play softball or anything. Right away Benjamin started racing around the black-top, yelling and acting like his usual wacko self. With a sigh, I dashed in front of him, letting him chase me.

At the end of the blacktop, I whirled on him. He skidded to a stop.

"Whoa! Almost got slimed! Get the Raid! Call the Cootie Busters — "

I leaned close to his face. "Shut your big mouth and listen. There's a plan to get back at the high school kids. If the plan works, they'll never pick on us again."

"What plan? What are you babbling about, Granville?"

I launched into my spiel. Benjamin's eyes narrowed skeptically when I told him about our secret Sixth-Grade Leader.

"Who's the leader? How come it's not me?" he demanded.

"Because you're not smart enough to think up an idea like this," I said. Outwardly I was cool but inside I was nervous. Benjamin Potter was going to be difficult. More than anyone, I needed him on the team. "If you were the last person on earth, I wouldn't pick you to be on this mission. But our Leader wants you. I'm just following orders."

"I don't believe you, Granville," he jeered. "I think this secret leader stuff is a crock."

"Think what you like. I'm glad you're not going to be one of us. But" — I paused craftily — "don't come crying to me when the rest of us are sixth-grade celebrities. You had your chance and you blew it." I turned to go.

"Hey, wait!"

I waited.

"How dangerous is this so-called plan?" he asked.

"Very," I replied. "If we're caught, we could all get suspended. Maybe even expelled."

"Really?" His face brightened. Only Benjamin would cheer up at the prospect of being thrown out of school. "Okay. I'm in. Take me to your leader. Ha! Ha!"

"Save your jokes," I told him crisply. "We meet tomorrow during recess. Don't say a word about this to anybody."

"Will the leader be there?"

"No. The leader's identity won't be revealed until D-Day." I turned to leave again.

"This had better not be a crock," Benjamin yelled after me. "Or you're dead, Granville."

If the plan didn't work, we would *all* be dead.

The express truck pulled up to the delivery entrance. I saw it from the windowed tower and nearly fainted with relief. If the shipment had been early or delayed, even by one day, the plan would have failed before it got started.

"This has to be it," I told Ellen, who was with me. We'd been watching for the truck the past two days.

"It may not be," she said. "It could be stuff for the dance." Below us, the Centerfest decorating committee was stringing lights in the atrium.

"No, look! See those boxes? This is it!" I grabbed her arm excitedly. A man opened the back of the truck and carefully unloaded small cartons.

"Now all we have to do is get Ms. Terry to let us help unpack them," I said.

"She won't," Ellen said gloomily.

But she did. As it turned out, the Centreville High teacher who was in charge of the ESC for the older students was looking for volunteers to help uncrate the laboratory shipment. Preparations for the dance had the high school kids totally wired. Nobody wanted to fool with crickets and lizards.

Ellen and I received permission to stay after school and work in the ESC. Ms. Terry contacted our mothers.

"I'm glad you girls are taking an interest in science," Ms. Terry said to us as she walked us upstairs to the lab.

"Well, we love feeding Garcia," I said. I hated deceiving Ms. Terry. She was a great teacher. But she couldn't prevent Benjamin and the others from picking on Ellen, no matter how often she punished them. And she couldn't make the older kids stop treating the sixth-graders like insects. We had to do that ourselves.

The lab teacher was named Mrs. Englehart.

"I can't thank you girls enough for helping out," she said when Ms. Terry left. "Wouldn't you know the shipment would arrive the day of the school's biggest social event?" She laughed. "I envisioned myself staying here all night, getting our little friends settled."

"How many little friends are there?" I asked Mrs. Englehart.

She checked a form lying on the counter. "Seventy-five chameleons. Three hundred crickets."

"Three hundred!" I cried. "Isn't that an awful lot?"

"Well, they all won't have survived the journey. Last year when I ordered chameleons and crickets, we had an early cold spell. The post office didn't inform me the poor things were sitting outside on a dock until it was too late. This time I decided to have them shipped directly to the school. Shall we get to work?"

She showed Ellen and me how to slit the cricket cartons. The insects were housed in plastic containers with holes in the top. The crickets looked a little groggy as we transferred them to their new homes, but Mrs. Englehart assured us they would perk up soon. I hoped so. Sleepy crickets would wreck our plan.

Mrs. Englehart uncrated the lizards herself. The chameleons were moved to big cages, several to a cage. My palms were slick with sweat. It was time for the crucial part of the plan.

"Ellen and I can finish up here," I said to Mrs. Englehart. "If you have some papers to grade . . . or something."

"I do have things to do in my office. Let me know when you're through. I'll walk you down to the entrance." She smiled. "Your teacher said you were very reliable young ladies. She's right."

If only she knew! Mrs. Englehart disappeared into the next room, leaving us alone with seventy-five chameleons and a couple of hundred crickets. After uncrating the rest of the crickets, we stacked all the cartons in the adjoining cleanup room.

One by one we shut the cage doors. Ellen looked as nervous as I felt.

"Oh, my gosh, look at the clock!" I said loudly. "Ellen, your mother is picking us up in exactly three minutes. Mrs. Englehart, we have to go now!"

The teacher came out of her office with a briefcase. "I was ready to leave myself," she said. She snapped off the purple grow lamps over the plants and the tube lights over the fish tanks. "They'll get plenty of daylight over the weekend," she remarked, closing the door behind her.

Downstairs, Ellen's mother waited by the curb in the Dietzler family car. Before we climbed in, Ellen clutched my arm.

"Maxie, do you realize what we've done?"

"Nothing, yet. Not really."

"But we *are* going to go through with it. I've never done anything like this in my whole life."

I was hardly the sneaky type myself. I tried to make my smile reassuring. "It'll be okay."

Confident words, but my bravery was temporary. Maxie the mole wanted to climb inside a long dark tunnel where it was safe.

11

Todd, are you going to stay in there all night? I have to get my toothbrush." I banged on the bathroom door again. "Todd? Are you alive in there?"

You'd have thought my brother actually had a date for the dance, for all the time he'd spent barricaded in the bathroom getting ready. Even though Todd couldn't get a date, he was going to the dance. "It's perfectly acceptable for freshmen to go stag," he said at the dinner table earlier. "Anyway, I'm on the entertainment committee. I have to make sure things run okay. I suppose you'll watch TV tonight," he added smugly to me.

Our truce at home was an uneasy one. I still hadn't forgiven him for shutting me in his locker. Now, however, I wished he'd let me in the bathroom.

"Todd, I'd like to get to Ellen's house sometime before midnight!"

The door opened suddenly, and my brother emerged in a cloud of steam. His face looked very pink, and he reeked of Dad's aftershave.

"You used Daddy's razor!" I shrieked. "Now I know why you were in there so long. You couldn't find a hair to shave!"

"Buzz off." He brushed past me, gassing me with the fumes of Old Spice. I pretended to swoon as Mom came around the corner with Todd's suit on a hanger.

"Maxie, if you're going to Ellen's, you'd better hurry," she said.

"I'm *try*ing, but the Master kept me waiting." I went inside and took my toothbrush from the holder. "Look at this mess! If I wrecked the bathroom like this, you'd kill me!"

Mom clucked her tongue. "Oh, well. It's his first dance, Maxie. He's nervous, poor kid."

"Poor kid" came bellowing down the hall, "Mom, will you fix my tie? It's too short or something."

I laughed. "You look like you're choking."

Todd frowned at me over Mom's shoulder as she expertly reknotted his tie. "Don't you have someplace to go?"

"As a matter of fact I do," I replied loftily. "And it'll be a lot more fun than any stale dance." I skipped into my room to finish packing my overnight bag.

At the door, I called, " 'Bye, Mom. 'Bye, Dad. See you tomorrow morning."

Mom came into the living room to kiss me good-bye. "Behave yourself at Ellen's house. Mind your manners."

"I will. 'Bye, everybody." I left with a semi-clear conscience: I *would* behave myself at Ellen's house. But I couldn't keep that promise *outside* of Ellen's house.

As part of the plan, I had arranged to spend the night at Ellen's house. That way, we'd both have an alibi. I jumped on my bike and pedaled furiously down her street. I needed to arrive at Centreville High before my brother did. If he caught a glimpse of his little sister, the cat would be out of the bag.

Mrs. Dietzler greeted me at the door. "Hello, Maxie. Just set your bag down there, dear. I'll take it back to Ellen's room later."

Ellen appeared, her cheeks pinker than Todd's. I know *she* didn't shave — her color was from sheer excitement. "Come on, Mom," she said anxiously. "We don't want to be late for the first act."

"I've never heard of a play starting at seven-twenty," Mrs. Dietzler said as we went out to her car. Ellen and I had cooked up a story so her mother would drive us to the school, no questions asked. Ellen's mother didn't realize the Centrefest

141

dance was taking place tonight. She thought we were going to see *Cheaper by the Dozen*.

In the backseat, Ellen whispered to me, "I hate fibbing to my mother."

"I know," I whispered back. "But it's not a complete fib. We *are* going to a play, sort of."

"Maxie, I'm scared. Suppose it doesn't work?"

"It will."

I knew exactly how Ellen felt, though. All the night before and that day I kept having panic attacks. What was a sensible, realistic person like me doing in the middle of a wild scheme like this? I must be out of my mind. But the plan was already in motion. We couldn't stop now.

At Centreville High, lights blazed from the atrium. Cars lined the bus loading zone. Girls in formal dresses teetered up the walkway in their high heels, on the arms of guys in tuxes or suits.

"My," Mrs. Dietzler remarked. "Quite a crowd for a play. Why are the students so dressed up? It looks more like a dance."

I thought fast. "The drama club told everybody to dress up for the first night. You know, like a Hollywood premiere?"

Mrs. Dietzler laughed. "Kids today are so sophisticated! Well, have a good time, you two. Your father will pick you up at ten, Ellen, so be out front."

Ellen and I scrambled out of the car. More couples were arriving every second. We had to sneak into the school undetected.

"They'll throw us out," Ellen said in a worried tone. "We aren't dressed up. We stick out like a couple of sore thumbs."

"Not if we go in with enough kids around us." I scanned the the entrance. "See that girl in the poufy blue dress? And the one in red beside her? We'll slip in with them. Follow me."

Getting into the school was actually very simple. Ticket-takers guarded the doors, but because the dance was being held in the atrium, all the doors were open and couples milled in and out without any restrictions. Nobody noticed two sixth-graders in jeans scurrying down the hall and up the stairs.

On the second floor, we leaned daringly over the glass-block wall. Below, the band members were tuning their instruments. At the other end of the atrium, teachers poured punch into huge bowls. Couples strolled hand in hand, waiting for the dance to officially begin.

The atrium was beautiful. The windowed wall of the Media Center was masked with leaf-printed panels. Tiny twinkling lights outlined the length of the lobby. Potted plants blocked unsightly doors. Autumn-hued balloons bobbled from the light fixtures, and everywhere there were bunches of yellow, orange, and scarlet paper leaves. Even though it was unseasonably warm outside, it was a fall fantasy inside.

"It's so beautiful," Ellen murmured. "It seems a shame to ruin it." She turned to me with troubled eyes. "Maxie, suppose this plan backfires? I mean, the high school kids may never forgive us for wrecking their dance."

"Remember the Boston Tea Party in history? The British were furious, but it showed the British the colonists meant business. Besides," I added, pulling her away before we were seen, "there'll be other dances."

Ellen was so sensitive. She worried constantly about hurting people's feelings, when nobody — except me and Ms. Terry — cared the least bit about Ellen's feelings.

Checking my watch, I said, "You'd better hide. The others will be here in a few minutes."

Ellen turned reluctantly from the fairy-tale scene below. "Where am I going to hide?"

"We could put you in a locker, but that's been done a lot lately," I said dryly. "I know. Behind the free-standing lockers. It's kind of dark back there. That'll make your entrance even more mysterious."

Ellen slipped into the shadows. "Do you think they'll all show up?" Her voice sounded hollow and metallic behind the lockers.

"They'd better." I took up my command post near the stairs, so I could tell when the others arrived.

"Maybe they won't be able to get in." Ellen worried a thousand times more than I did.

Music blared upward. I peeped over the half-wall. The dance seemed to be in full swing. "They shouldn't have any problem. All the doors are open. Ellen, quit worrying. You're the Sixth-Grade Leader, remember?"

"I feel more like the Sixth-Grade Guinea Pig."

I laughed, mostly to ease my own nervous tension. At last I heard footsteps scrunching up the steps.

"Somebody's coming! Stay back till I tell you," I alerted Ellen. I shrank into the shadows, my legs quivering. If it was a teacher, I'd have to have some kind of a story ready. But my brain was mush!

A blonde head appeared. Then two. Katherine and Michelle ran lightly onto the landing. I breathed an enormous sigh of relief.

"Over here!" I raised my voice to be heard over the band.

Katherine squinted into the dimness. "Maxie? Is that you?"

"Yeah, it's me." I stepped into the light. "Where's Michael? And Benjamin?

"I don't know." Katherine gazed down at the dance. "Michelle, look! Isn't this cool?"

"Get back, you guys. Somebody might see you." I herded them to my corner.

"Where's our mysterious leader?" Michelle giggled. I hoped they would get serious. I needed help I could depend on, or we'd all wind up suspended.

"You'll meet our leader when we're all here," I said. "Pipe down, will you?"

"Nobody can hear us," Katherine said. "Not over the music."

I glanced around anxiously. "Those boys had better show up — "

In our meeting, I only relayed the schedule for the Big Night, no details. I was taking a chance on their curiosity. The less they knew, I figured, the greater the surprise element.

Just then two figures emerged at the top of the stairs. Both wore camouflage pants and dark hooded sweatshirts, like commando raiders. Michelle squealed and grabbed my arm. I was scared myself, until I recognized Benjamin Potter's tubby silhouette. Michael spotted us huddled against the wall.

"There they are," he said to Benjamin.

Benjamin stomped over. "Okay, we're here, Granville. What's this great plan you wouldn't tell us yesterday? And where's this mysterious leader?"

"Yeah," Michelle said, "Where is Dilys? Is she hiding?"

I told them the rest of the plan. In the half-light I could see Michelle's eyes were like dinner plates. Katherine popped her gum wordlessly. Benjamin let out a long low whistle, then grinned at Michael. "All right!" he cried. "Bring on the genius who thought this up!"

They were definitely impressed by the plan, but would they be equally impressed by Ellen's dramatic entrance? Only one way to find out.

Lifting my voice in the direction of the lockers, I said, "Come on out and meet your loyal followers."

Ellen took so long to appear I was afraid she'd sneaked down the back stairs. Finally a figure strode regally out of the shadows. The ceiling lights revealed Ellen's face, pale but perfectly composed. Her shoulders were squared and her fists were clenched, ready for battle. She looked every inch a general.

The others were awestruck. Ellen Dietzler was absolutely the last person on earth they had expected to see. Benjamin was the first to recover.

"Her?" he sneered. "Slimeball Dietzler? *She*

thought up that great plan? *I'm* not her loyal follower!"

I knew this would happen, and I had a speech all prepared, but suddenly Ellen spoke.

Drawing herself up to her full height, she regarded Benjamin levelly. "Yes, me. If you don't like it, Potter, you can get out right now. There's a lot riding on this plan. Everybody here could get suspended. I don't want any cowards messing it up for the others. I picked you guys because I thought you had guts."

I nearly fell over. Ellen certainly didn't need *me* defending her!

"I'm not a coward," Benjamin denied. "I'm braver than anybody here — "

"Then be quiet and do as you're told," Ellen snapped. I was flabbergasted. How come Ellen had never stood up to him before? Maybe, I thought slowly, because she had never been in a position of authority before. As the Sixth-Grade Leader, Ellen was certainly living up to the title.

"Anybody else want to back out?" Ellen said, looking at each of us in turn. "Now's your chance."

"I don't know — " Michelle said doubtfully.

Katherine poked her in the ribs. "Aw, come on. We'll never be able to do anything like this again. It's a perfect setup." She glared at Benjamin. "Let the boys back out. The *girls* can do it."

Even though I didn't get along that well with Katherine, I could have hugged her. She was on Ellen's side! And if Katherine accepted Ellen, Michelle would, too. Only the boys — really, just Benjamin — held out. Michael hadn't said a word, either for or against.

"I'm not backing out!" Benjamin said. "I've got plenty of guts!"

"You can say that again," Katherine giggled.

Michael cast the deciding vote. "Are we going to do this or not?" he said.

"Okay," Ellen said. "Does everybody here have an alibi?"

They did. Katherine and Michelle were supposed to be at the movies. Benjamin had told his mother that he was with Michael, and Michael had told his mother he was with Benjamin.

"Okay, you know the drill. Let's go." Ellen wheeled, heading for the stairs to the third floor.

It was creepy on the third floor. Ellen went directly to the ESC and opened the door. Fortunately lights from the stadium outside poured in through the windows, so we could see without switching on an overhead light. Ellen led us to the cartons we'd piled in the cleanup room.

"Grab a bunch of cartons, everybody," she ordered. "Benjamin, you and Michael pack the lizards. We'll empty the cricket cages."

"Ewwww!" Michelle said. "I'm glad I don't have to touch those awful lizards!"

Benjamin had trouble capturing the lizards at first. Soon he and Michael developed a system to catch the lightning-fast creatures.

The crickets had come to life in their new surroundings and hopped out of our reaching hands like corn popping. We couldn't get them all — some of the crickets hid in the grass and leaves that lined their cages. But we had enough to do the job.

Ellen divided the cartons among the six of us. Scritchings inside the cardboard boxes told us the crickets and lizards were raring to go. So were we.

Ellen grouped us into teams of two. Michelle and Katherine, Benjamin and Michael, and me and Ellen. "There are three halls that lead to the atrium," she instructed. "We'll each take a hall. When you finish unloading, don't hang around. Bail out. It'll be every man for himself. Good luck."

"We'll need it," Michelle muttered, stacking her cartons in her arms.

I thought so, too, now that the hour was upon us, as they say in movies. I picked up my own cartons. With Ellen in the lead, we crept down the back stairs. At the bottom of the steps, we split up. Ellen and I took the hallway nearest the cafeteria, where the band was set up.

The lamps in the atrium had been dimmed, except for the starry white lights. Dancers shuffled to a slow number.

Crouching on the floor, we quickly opened our cartons.

"Shoo!" I commanded my crickets and lizards. "Scat!"

The crickets didn't need any encouragement. They boinged onto the dance floor. The lizards seemed rather sluggish. I nudged a few and they scuttled forward. I rocked back on my heels and waited for the fireworks to begin.

It didn't take long. Soon the dance floor was alive with insects and reptiles! Girls screamed, frantically brushing crickets off their formal dresses. The scene was pandemonium as crickets leaped between dancers and lizards darted between their feet. The couples looked like they were doing a Mexican hat dance!

I started laughing. Beside me, Ellen was cracking up, too.

One of the teachers next to the punch bowls rushed into the fray, shouting, "Who's responsible for this? Where did those bugs come from? Where is the entertainment committee?"

Ellen plucked my sleeve. "Come on, Maxie. We'd better get out of here."

The last thing I saw before leaving was my brother, who was on the entertainment committee. Todd crawled clumsily around on the floor in his good suit, grabbing at crickets but mostly nabbing air.

It was a sight to remember for the rest of my life!

12

Monday morning, the whole school was in an uproar over the dance. I warned Ellen that this would probably happen. "Keep a straight face. Act like it's all news to you."

When I walked into the atrium, the first thing I saw was a chameleon inching nonchalantly up the Centreville Wildcat mural. Its tail was blue, to match the mural. Evidently Todd and the other members of the entertainment committee had had a hard time rounding up the entire population of lizards and crickets.

I'd heard all about "the fiasco" from Todd when I got home from Ellen's house Saturday. He was furious because he'd kept getting his fingers stepped on trying to capture slippery lizards. When the girls finally stopped screeching, Todd reported bitterly, they began to laugh. It *was* funny, though my brother failed to see the humor in the situation. The band played an old rock song called "Bungle in the Jungle," which didn't help matters any. Zany "Speed," the skateboard wizard, had suddenly become stodgy.

"You didn't hurt them, did you?" I asked my brother.

"Hurt what, those bugs? Have you ever tried to catch a hundred million crickets?"

Yes, I nearly said.

I was relieved the high school kids thought the whole thing was funny. We didn't intend to ruin their dance — just let them know the sixth-graders were part of the school, not "boarders." That half of the plan still had to come off, so it wasn't over for the members of the Bug Squad. Not yet.

In room 228, I avoided looking at Michelle, Katherine, Michael, and Benjamin. They avoided looking at me, too. If we started giggling, Ms. Terry would become suspicious. Ellen dared to shoot me a grin across the room. She seemed bubbly and happy, not her usual shy self at all.

Dilys stared at me. "I tried to call you this weekend. Your mother said you were at Ellen's house."

"I was." Instead of asking Dilys what she wanted — something the old Maxie would do — I added cheerfully, "We had a great time. Ellen's a lot of fun, once you get to know her."

"Did you hear about the dance?"

"Yeah. Todd was there. It must have been a riot. I wish I could have seen those bugs jumping all over the place."

"My mother has an expression," Dilys said. " 'Still waters run deep.' "

"What does that mean?"

"It means that quiet people sometimes do surprising things."

This was the longest conversation Dilys and I had had in weeks. "Like who, for instance?"

"Like Ellen Dietzler, for instance."

I wondered who'd let it slip, Katherine or Michelle? "True," I said. "Ellen isn't who you think she is."

"I'm not sure you are, either."

"Oh, I'm just plain old me," I said with exaggerated modesty.

Ms. Terry called the roll, ending our discussion. But Dilys kept glancing at me during math, giving me interested, quizzical looks — as if she weren't sure who she'd been sitting next to all this time.

At lunchtime, we learned that the four assistant principals visited each homeroom and grilled the high school students. No one owned up to swiping the lizards and crickets from the ESC and letting them loose on the dance floor.

The six of us — Benjamin, Michael, Katherine,

Michelle, Ellen, and me — sat at one end of the table, a first in the history of the sixth grade. Boys never sat next to girls and Ellen had never been allowed to sit next to anyone. The other kids noticed and began whispering. The teachers didn't pay any attention to this unusual arrangement. They were probably thrilled that Ellen was no longer an outsider.

"Do you think the principal will come to our rooms?" Michael asked, concerned.

"Nah." Benjamin chomped his bologna sandwich, squirting mustard on his chin. No wonder girls didn't want to sit with boys. "How could they accuse us? Little kids weren't supposed to be at their dance." He grinned, baring mustard-yellow teeth.

"He's right," I said. "They'll never suspect us. Just like nobody will ever suspect Ellen as our leader. That's why we had to keep her identity secret until the night of the dance."

"That was sure a surprise," Katherine remarked. To Ellen she said, "How did you ever think up such a great idea?"

With a smile at me, Ellen replied, "It just came to me."

"Well somebody *had* to stick up for us sixth-graders," I put in hastily, not wanting to spoil Ellen's moment of glory. It was important for Ellen to have *all* the credit for the plan. I didn't mind not sharing the spotlight. Inside I knew I wasn't anybody's assistant. Not anymore.

Michelle took a dreamy sip of milk. "Like Joan of Arc. You remind me of her." Ellen blushed.

"Hold on," Benjamin said. "If we have to keep this a big secret, how will the older kids know it was *us* that did it?"

"They'll find out," I said, wishing Benjamin had brought a napkin. Not that he'd use it. I twisted in my seat. Dilys was sitting at the freshman table with her friends. They were all talking excitedly. "All we have to do is wait." I crossed my fingers hopefully.

One time we were watching an old war movie on cable where people passed messages from town to town without alerting the bad guys. Dad told us that method of communication was called an "underground." I was counting on the underground to spread the word that it was the sixth-graders, not a bunch of older kids, who had "livened" up the dance.

We didn't have to wait long, either. Student underground was a lot faster than any interrogation by assistant principals.

On the way out of the cafeteria, I was stopped by Dilys' ninth-grade friend, Gail. She wore her red hair in a sort of whale spout on top of her head, and a million strands of glass beads around her neck.

"Dilys thinks you sixth-graders were at the dance," Gail said bluntly. "Is it true? Did you let all those crickets and lizards loose?"

"Would we do a thing like that?" I said innocently. "Us little Munchkins?"

Gail shrieked with laughter. She slapped me on the back so hard I nearly fell over. "You kids are all right! Shake up the establishment, go for it!"

She left with the other ninth-grade drama students. They all had on weird outfits. No wonder Dilys preferred the older kids to me. They had a lot in common.

"What did she mean, 'shake up the establishment'?" Ellen asked.

I shrugged. "Who knows? Maybe she didn't have a date for the dance."

"Who'd date *her*?" Benjamin held his nose. "*I* wouldn't."

"She's probably thanking her lucky stars this very minute," Ellen said, laughing. Katherine and Michelle laughed, too.

Benjamin said, with a snort of disgust, "Girls!" and stumped off. But I could tell he was going to leave Ellen alone from now on. Since Friday night, things had definitely changed.

Back upstairs, Ms. Terry informed us that our ESC privileges had been taken away for a week, until the rest of the fugitive lizards and crickets were rounded up.

Ellen raised her hand. "Who's going to feed Garcia?" she asked the teacher. Her face was absolutely expressionless. If Ms. Terry suspected Ellen in the least, she would not expect her to voluntarily continue the discussion of the ESC. A guilty kid would let the subject pass without calling attention to herself. Ellen was very smart.

Ms. Terry replied, "How thoughtful of you to think of the rabbit, Ellen. Mrs. Englehart will take care of him. Now, let's get out our spelling books."

Chir-eep! Chir-eep!

The sound came from the top of the blackboard. Everyone giggled. One of the crickets was still at large.

"I hope a lizard isn't hiding under my chair," Ms. Terry said good-naturedly. I decided then and there that Ms. Terry was one of us. If I lived to be a hundred, I would never have another teacher as great as Ms. Terry. And she would probably never have another class like ours!

I was backing my bicycle out of the garage when a shadow blocked the late November sunshine slanting across the cement floor. I whirled around, making sure the hem of my sweatshirt covered what I had tucked in the waistband of my jeans.

It was Dilys. She hadn't been over to my house in weeks. She looked the same as she did in school. Weird, unmatched clothes. Her bangs needed cutting.

"Going out?" she asked unnecessarily.

I swung my leg over the seat. "Yeah. Ellen and I are going bike riding. We're meeting Katherine and Michelle at the mall."

Dilys slouched against the wall of the garage, as if she had all the time in the world. "I haven't had frozen yogurt since last summer."

"Well, they still make it." I gripped the handlebars tightly. "What do you want, Dilys? You came over here for a reason."

She sighed. "I had a feeling the small-talk approach wouldn't work."

"Work for what?"

"Maxie — " She hesitated, fiddling with the zippers that trimmed her shirt. The shirt looked like something out of a seventies disco movie. Dilys was still buying her clothes at the thrift shop.

"What?" I demanded. "What do you *want*, Dilys?"

"I want us to be friends again."

If she had said those words two months ago, I would have been thrilled to pieces. How many nights had I tossed and turned, wishing and hoping Dilys would get bored with Gail's crowd and things would go back to normal? But too much had happened since Dilys had dumped me. I said, "I guess you finally got tired of Gail and the drama crew."

Dilys smiled sheepishly and brushed aside her long bangs. "Actually, they got tired of me. They're busy with the Christmas production. I guess — I think I was sort of a passing fling for them."

"A mascot," I supplied.

"Yeah. I wasn't really one of them," Dilys admitted. "More like their pet."

"Gee, that's too bad." I kept my tone neutral. What did Dilys want me to do? Fall on my knees and beg to be best friends again?

A silence stretched between us. Then Dilys said, "It's amazing the way the big kids treat us now, isn't it? No more Munchkin Pats or calling us names . . . we're really part of the school."

"Yes, thanks to Ellen." All the sixth-graders knew that Ellen Dietzler was responsible for the Centerfest fiasco. She was the hero of the Willow Springs Annex.

"You really like Ellen, don't you?" Dilys asked. "Is she your best friend now? I notice you always wear that bracelet she gave you."

The question threw me off-guard. "She's a good

161

friend. But I don't really have a best friend anymore."

"I don't, either." Then Dilys seemed to understand what I meant. "I guess you don't want to be friends with me, ever again."

"I never said that."

She looked at me hopefully. "Then we *can* be friends, just like before."

"We can be friends." I let it go at that.

Dilys and I could never be friends the way we were before. I wasn't the dull, molelike follower anymore. I had changed. All of us had changed. But it was inevitable — we were going to high school now. It was bound to happen.

"Want to come with us?" I offered. "I'm biking over to Ellen's house, and then we're riding to the mall."

Dilys' face lit up. "I haven't ridden my bike in *ages*. It'll be just like last summer again! Wait, I have to put on jeans. I won't be a second. Come over to my house and wait for me."

Two months ago I would have tagged along after Dilys at the drop of a hat.

I shook my head. "I'll be over at Ellen's. We'll wait for you there."

As Dilys sprinted across the lawn to her house, I watched her, one foot resting on the pedal. What would it be like to be friends with Dilys again?

Would she try to take over, the way she always had? I was glad Dilys and I weren't enemies anymore, but this time things would be different. We wouldn't be linked exclusively together. Ellen, Michelle, Katherine, and I got along fine. Dilys would have to conform a little if she wanted to fit in with our group. And I could tell her from experience that it was no fun being friendless.

The back door banged.

"Hey, Moondoggie, posing for a statue?" Todd coasted down the driveway on his skateboard. He carried a bag of garbage.

I laughed. Only Todd took out the garbage on a skateboard. Since his team had won the track meet, he was in seventh heaven. Mom said high school really agreed with him. I think it might finally be agreeing with me, too.

Pulling the green spiral notebook from the waistband of my jeans, I uncapped my felt-tip pen with my teeth.

"What are you doing, taking a census?" Todd asked, carving figure eights around the garbage bag. He twirled the yellow twist-tie like a miniature baton.

"Never mind, nosy."

Todd flipped his skateboard with one foot. Now that he was a big track star, he was zany old "Speed" again. He'd never know I'd got back at him for closing me in his locker. Maybe I'd drop him a little hint.

"Watchoutthere'salizard!" I cried.

"Where?" The skateboard flew out from under him. Todd caught himself in time.

I giggled. "Scared of lizards, Toddie?"

"If I never see one of the critters again it'll be too soon." He stopped rolling to stare at me. "Rumor has it that some sixth-graders let those bugs and lizards loose at the dance. You wouldn't happen to know anything about it, would you?"

"Who, me?" I said, super-innocent. "Would I do anything like that?"

"Why not? It's your school."

"Not my school."

"Yeah, *your* school," he insisted.

"I thought we were just boarders. What was it you called us? Tenants?"

"Well, think of this year as a trial run," Todd said. "When you get to Centreville High for real in three years, it'll be like old home week."

He was right. After this year, high school ought to be a breeze. In three years, they'd still be talking about the night the sixth-graders raided the dance. My class would be remembered for a long time.

I scribbled my last theory of life. It wasn't even my own personal theory. I borrowed it from my mother.

Take life one day at a time.

Closing my notebook, I pedaled down the curb. "Don't close that garbage bag," I said to my brother. "I have to put something in it."

He watched as I dropped in my *Theory of Life*, Vol. II, notebook. "That looks important. Are you sure you want to throw that whole notebook away?"

"Positive. I don't need it anymore."

Then I cut a mean figure eight on my bike before racing off to Ellen's house.

About the Author

CANDICE F. RANSOM lives in Centreville, Virginia, with her husband and black cat. She writes books for young people and enjoys going out to eat whenever she can.

Her popular Kobie books are based on her own experiences growing up. Ms. Ransom says, "My brain stops at about age fifteen. I'm a grown-up by default." Some of her other books include, *My Sister, the Meanie; My Sister, the Traitor; My Sister, the Creep;* and *Millicent the Magnificent.*

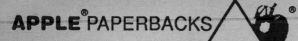